Sira

    Sira groaned; she had been staring at a blank page for hours. She hadn't come up with a character, not a shred of plot, and not an inkling of setting. Tireless hours she had exercised her brain with books, help videos, and advice from other writers. Nothing. Fruitless efforts. Her inspiration just went kaput every time she sat down.
    Of course; the week before her creative writing assignment was due, Sira hadn't even been able to start. By contrast, her friend, Zach, had been able to compose a 20,000-word novella in a mere two weeks. He was always better at stuff than Sira.
    Her head began to hurt. Rubbing her temples, Sira checked the clock: 11:52 PM. Sighing, she picked out her pajamas and shambled to the bathroom to change. Taking off her shirt, she contemplated whether she should shower so late or just wake up early and shower before Seminary. Considering she tended to take long showers, Sira decided that a late-night shower would be better than an early morning one.
    Several minutes later found her lost in thought, the hot water cascading over her every curve. Her fingers ran through her pixie cut hair, light brown and streaked with highlights. Sira was slender, but not particularly muscular. At fourteen, she was taller than most her age, which was fine with her, since she didn't get out much.
    Sighing, Sira finished scrubbing and turned off the shower. Rather than use an obscenely loud hairdryer, she brushed out the tangles and pulled it all into a short ponytail. Now changed into comfortable pajamas, Sira stretched and examined her face.
    Around her bright blue eyes and small nose, some new, small, red bumps had formed. Of course there was another outbreak. Just another thing to be worried about. She rolled her eyes and snuck out of the bathroom to bed. Sira conducted her nightly routine; praying, reading in her Scriptures, and then journaling. After that, she shut off the light, turned on a reading lamp and got out the book she was reading.
    Gradually, Sira progressed through the book, analyzing the plot and characters. She was reading it because it was her favorite author,

but this, as well, had yet to yield fruit. Eventually, her consciousness drifted. She dipped into sleep and, from her world, at least, Sira flew far away.

She felt like she was falling, as she often did at the end of one of her dreams. Sira opened her eyes and yelped in surprise. Above her was sky, crisp and blue, with scattered clouds. The wind was rushing past her and she couldn't feel anything beneath her. Sira rolled over and somehow managed not to pass out; the ground below her was fast approaching. She let out a pitiful whimper and closed her eyes again, panic welling up in her chest.

Suddenly, something hit her side and her trajectory changed, now at a gentler speed. She had a sense of someone carrying her. Opening her eyes, she still saw sky, but when she turned her head away from the wind... wow.

Sira's rescuer was beautiful. She - they - it was very puzzling, but magnificent. Its face appeared that of a woman's, but shifted constantly, even showing masculine traits at times, leaving Sira uncertain what to call this creature. She decided to focus elsewhere.

The creature's hair flowed behind it, inky black and flecked with bright points of light, like the Milky Way, but there were no constellations in there. At least, not any that Sira recognized. The being had a pair of large wings, which undulated gingerly, their black feathers rustling in the descent. The dress - or perhaps, robe - that it was wearing was excessively long. If it was on the ground, it could easily pass for a wedding train. How such a piece of clothing could be considered practical, Sira had no idea.

The creature, fair and mysterious noticed Sira observing it and promptly spoke, the voice resonant and as fluid as its bearer's face, "You judge me, even though I rescued you?"

Sira was intimidated and, as a result, couldn't find the words to respond.

The creature laughed, "That is all right, child. And do not worry, I will put you down safely."

Sure enough, their flight downwards was gradual and soft, like a feather shed from a wing. The creature hovered a few inches above the terrain and set Sira down lightly.

"Take a look around you." The creature commanded.

Obeying, Sira glanced around at the strange place they had landed in. They stood on a hilltop, which was covered in waving, red grass, as was most of the plateau around them. On one side of the hill, thin trees sprouted a wide, thin canopy of red leaves. On the other, a small lake was split in two by a sort of peninsula. Beyond that, a rocky cliff fell away out of sight, joining the land below. Far away, Sira could just make out a line of mountains marching... south, by the position of what she believed was the sun. But everything she saw, Sira felt it was a little... off. In her head, there was something that needed to be filled in, but... there was no telling what it was. And where was this place? Nowhere on earth had red grass that she knew of. And it felt like the middle of summer, so why were all the leaves red?

Why was she here? Shouldn't she be getting back? Was this all a dream? If this was a dream, how come it felt so real? Was she a living cliché? Sira asked herself all of these questions and couldn't even begin to answer one of them. She turned to the creature, who was staring patiently at her. "Which would you ask first? You get four and I get four."

Eight. Strange. Usually, it's seven or three or thirteen or something auspicious like that. Four questions. Sira would have to choose carefully, obviously, "Where am I?"

"A different world than yours. One that is in peril and one that can only be visited by those who seek to be complete. In other, simpler words, this world is Dream, or Rest, or Memory; whichever you prefer."

That just gave Sira MORE questions, but she still had more pressing ones, "Who and what are you?"

It laughed again, "Two questions, but one sentence. Very well, I will answer both at no extra expense. I am Anima, a female, since I can tell you are confused about that. I am a higher being in this world, only able to descend briefly, such as situations like this."

"What do you want me to do?"

Anima turned gracefully and pointed over the forest, "Just past there is a village, where several like you will be waiting. Your last question?"

Thoughtfully, Sira replied, "When can I go back?" She was worried; it had taken a fall into Dream and Anima to rescue her and now, she was wondering more than when, but how. If Anima could only grace Dream with her presence every so often, then she would be stranded here.

The higher being smiled, "All that and more will be explained when you do what I ask. Now, I have a few questions for you."

In no mood to answer questions, but also feeling obligated, Sira reluctantly nodded her consent.

"Very good. Do you, perchance, know of the nature of the human mind during sleep?"

This took her by surprise; Sira had been expecting something deeper, not a science pop quiz. "Um… I know that dreams help process memories and experiences. But they're also influenced by thoughts?"

"And what do you know of psychological theories?"

"I… many people speculate that the human brain is developed through equal parts genetics and experiences, so even identical twins can't be exactly alike."

"And have you ever noticed your dreams taking on a certain pattern?"

Sira recalled a time where she had had a dream about a mundane experience and then, several months later, the dream had come true as precisely as it was predicted, "Yes, although, it only happens every once in a while."

"And my last question, what do you fear most?" Anima's tone was serious, almost dreadful.

Sira was even more taken aback now. She quickly called up what she was general scared of; heights, drowning, and, admittedly, the dark. They were good starts, but she couldn't think of why. Then it clicked. She was afraid of what would happen if she fell from a great height. She was afraid of her lungs and head crying out if she drowned. And lastly, she was afraid of what might reach out from the darkness and snatch her. All of these had one root: pain.

Anima must have been reading her thoughts, "Ah, so you have figured it out; the only fear that you have is a logical one, one to hold onto and to listen to. However, you must be willing to go against it if you know what you need to do."

Like most heroes that she had read of, Sira chose the logical response, "What does that mean?"

Anima was merely silent as she flapped her wings, ascending gracefully, yet sadly, as if she would miss her questionnaires. She continued to rise until she vanished in a flash of light, just like all benevolent beings.

Sira folded her arms and huffed ungratefully. Figures.

Of course, the goddess of the land would dump her in the middle of nowhere in a world that was supposedly in peril with naught so much as a stick to defend herself. She looked down and was somewhat relieved that Anima had changed Sira's mauve pajamas into a different outfit more, uh, suited for travel.

Her top was a sort of tight-fit black shirt with matching leather armor on the shoulders and right side of the chest. Her pants were black denim, but flexible and light, tucked into black combat boots. With her pixie cut, she speculated she looked like some kind of punk going to an edgy convention or rave or whatever.

Sighing heavily, Sira sat down in order to slow her brain and think for a moment. She had fallen asleep. She had been rescued by a shifty - quite literally - pretty "lady" with wings and cosmic hair who then proceeded to quiz her about her psychology knowledge like this whole new world wasn't in jeopardy. And, she needed to go west, through the forest of strange trees. Yeah, it made sense.

Just, the fact that everything was red, it hurt her eyes. It wasn't that it was too bright or anything, she just hated the color, not since... well, that wasn't important.

Regardless, Sira figured that she might as well follow through with Anima's orders. She stood up and glared once more toward the west horizon. Sure enough, she could just make out a wall with turrets. Hardly a village. More like a Renaissance city. If that passed as a village, Sira wondered what would be classified as a town. Or even a suburb. If Dream had suburbs.

Well, if she made it there alive, she would find out. But Sira, irked by the obscurity of Anima's words, strode carefully towards the woods, soon becoming swallowed by the grip of the light, ghostly shadows.

Chapter 2
Kyo

Woods. Darkness. Menacing noises. Kyo woke up to all of that. Naturally, his instinct was to run. Why did he run? He had no idea. He couldn't remember why. The only thing he could remember is waking up on his feet, afraid and in the dark. That and his name. And that this particular condition was called amnesia. And that it was a particularly overused plot device. How that was in his brain and not, say, an hour of his life, he had no idea. That was partially due to the scientific knowledge he felt was missing.

But anyway, he had woods, darkness, and menacing noises to run from in order to live. Having no time to examine his appearance, Kyo dashed for a small, orange point of light he saw. Perhaps a sunset?

As he got closer and realized it was flickering, he was disappointed. It was only a fire, though it appeared to be on the move. A torch, then. A torch meant another person, which meant civilization, which meant safety. Hearing a twig snap behind him, Kyo ran harder.

The torch was moving away from him, but slowly. Trying to get the bearer's attention, Kyo tried to yell, but couldn't find his voice. Somehow, though, the bearer of the torch seemed to hear him.

The torch stopped and soon enough, Kyo caught up to it. There was no bearer, the torch merely floated. He reached out cautiously, the nonsense of it screaming in his brain. The need for light was overwhelming, but he was wary of such a ready source. He pulled his hand back and kept running.

As he suspected, the light snuffed itself out and the eerie noises, which had faded before, resumed suddenly, crashing down upon him.

Kyo's fear consumed him, but he didn't scream. He couldn't. He only cried. And ran. And ran and ran and ran.

It was so dark, Kyo couldn't see anything, so when he ran into the tree at full force, he just collapsed, his head bleeding and throbbing worse than he'd ever felt, even though this was his first experience with pain.

Above him, two grotesque faces materialized, grinning upon his helpless figure. One, a human with the skin peeling off around his smile, threatened menacingly, "He would make a marvelous present for the Reaper."

The other, a vaguely canine head with large, decayed tusks, agreed with a hiss, "Yes, I can practically taste his Essence."

Kyo could sense the importance behind these words; the Reaper and this Essence were both new to him and familiar. And these... demons were wishing to sacrifice his Essence to the Reaper. That was never good. He knew he should get up and run, but he was paralyzed, but whether by fear or some sort of devilish magic, he didn't know. He could only lie in wait as the faces drew closer and their mouths opened wide.

The sound of a bow snapping rang out twice. Kyo could hear the arrows as they sang through the air and felt them as they clave through his would-be captors' skin and stopped just short of his own. Around him, the demons collapsed and dissolved and Kyo found he could move again.

Out of the darkness, from above in the trees and from ground level, two identical beings approached him. They joined to become one and it came to Kyo, reaching out its hand, "Well?" From the voice, Kyo decided it was a she, "Best not to take a nap in Nightmare."

He couldn't respond vocally, but Kyo took her hand and stood up. In the darkness, she almost seemed to glow. Her light brown hair resonated dimly and her young face produced its own light. She tilted her head to the side, "Stop staring; you might make some of the demons jealous."

Reflexively, Kyo starting waving his hands around intricately, but the girl just waved him off, "Don't worry, I won't bite. Y'know, much. Now come on."

And she took off. Not having anything better to do, Kyo followed, though just far enough away for her not to bite.

The demons had apparently given up all subtlety, since they attacked out of nowhere in a mad rage. Each time they appeared, Kyo's guide cut or shot them down, sometimes using her bow, others slashing with concealed knives on her forearms. Each time, she kept going without missing a beat, as if it were natural for her to take strolls in a purgatorial forest.

Kyo noticed the little things about her; her stride, the way she tensed before killing a demon, the little point on the side of her left ear, the important things like that. She looked like she was about twelve, but she ran like she was twenty, so Kyo could barely keep up.

Soon enough, however, her light started to become obsolete, as a new, much broader light source was becoming apparent; daylight. Simultaneously, the demons stopped their onslaught, either because such light was poisonous to them or the girl scared them. Kyo couldn't decide whether the latter would be better for him or not.

After so long in the dark, he had to squint for a bit until his eyes adjusted, which was pretty fast. All around him was red grass and sunlight. Behind him, in the forest Nightmare, the trees were all made of black wood and leaves, and the grass was dark brown, as if every organism in there hated light and boycotted it.

Ahead of Kyo, the girl was stretching and yawning, apparently unfazed by the strenuous activity she just endured, "Nothing like running for your life to wake up in the morning!" She turned back to him and reached out her hand. Kyo flinched, expecting a saber to jump into her fingers and threaten his carotid artery.

She laughed heartily, "Relax! I'm only a human. My name's Olivia, how 'bout yours?"

He shook her hand and opened his mouth to speak, but despite moving it to form his name, no sound came out.

"What's the matter, cat got your tongue?"

Kyo started to move his hands this time, but this time he understood why; he knew perfect sign language, which meant this was how he was used to communicating. He tried to explain this to Olivia, but she wouldn't hear it. So to speak.

"Oh, I get it, you're mute! That's all right. And this hand-waving thing won't be necessary. Here." She reached up and touched the side of Kyo's head and began to concentrate.

A sharp pain hit him right where she touched him, but it receded quickly. She opened her eyes and looked at him directly, Now, is that better?

He blinked. Her voice had just rung in his head. Kyo knew it was telepathy, but with no mental voice, would it still work?

Olivia messaged him again, *It's just telepathy, give it a try.*

Tentatively, Kyo imagined his thoughts reaching her, *My name's Kyo.* He could hear his "voice", but it sounded artificial, like a robot that was trying to sound human.

She laughed out loud and spoke, "Well, Kyo, you're awfully easy to communicate with."

But how did you-

"Establish a telepathic link? I've had some practice. And your Essence is super easy to touch magically. No wonder those demons were having so much fun with you."

There was that word again, Essence. Kyo, wanting to use this new telepathy as much as possible, could only ask, *What exactly is Essence? Is it, like, magic or something?*

Olivia paused for a moment, "I guess you could say that."

And the demons mentioned something else. The Reaper? They said my Essence would be perfect to give to it. Do you know what it is?

Her expression became guarded, and this time, her mouth didn't move, *You'd better come with me.*

She turned away and began to walk. Not wanting to be alone, Kyo hurried to catch up. He looked ahead, but they were surrounded by hills, *Where, exactly, are we going?*

"A village. Apparently, there's a lot going on that needs to be explained. Why that information isn't just implanted into the new recruit's brains, I have no idea."

New recruits?

Olivia imitated a higher accent that he didn't know, "'All this and more will be explained if you just follow my instructions.' Ugh, she gets on my nerves."

Obviously, Kyo had no idea how to respond, so he didn't.

She continued to converse, despite the silence, "I'm going to take your silence as an 'umm'. Don't worry, once we eventually get there, we'll try to tell you what we can."

They trudged to the top of the hill in silence. Once they reached the top, Kyo collapsed, a migraine rupturing his skull.

Olivia's voice was full of concern, "What is it? What's wrong?"

He couldn't focus enough to respond telepathically, but he knew the answer. He remembered something. The walled city, surrounded by a red forest. The city he grew up in. Kyo lived here. He lived in Dream.

Chapter 3
Therin

Yawning and stretching, Therin rolled out of bed. Just last night, a new girl had come into Daydream. Based on her modern attire, she naturally suspected that the newbie, Sira, was one of the last of six recruits, hence why she was sleeping in the same dorm building. And now, Olivia was on her way to find the very last. FINALLY, they would get to do something after waiting for forever.

Therin and her brother, Ryan, had come to Dream a couple weeks ago. Their instructions were to wait and develop their Essences. Supposedly, given time, the next recruits would be found. But secretly, Therin believed that Anima didn't have a plan. That this Reaper that they were supposed to fight scared the deity just as much as it did them.

When they had arrived, Olivia had already been here for a month or so and the other guy, who had only introduced himself as Dom, had resided in daydream for almost two years. Obviously, he was powerful by now, but he hardly ever used his Essence. Therin had tried to get him to show her some moves, but the teenager just declined her, going into his residence and sealing it off.

Regardless, while Olivia was having fun frolicking in Nightmare (which for some reason is a good place for a recruit to awaken), it was Therin's duty to get Sira up to speed. It was quite daunting, considering she was, like, three years older than Therin. Dom couldn't do it because he had to patrol the gates and Ryan was scouting, so… ugh. She just had to bide her time until Olivia got back. They were the same age, but Olivia was far more experienced than her.

Changing quickly, Therin slowly opened the door and quietly crept down the stairs. Maybe Sira wasn't awake yet. She reached the bottom and sighed. There was the noob, waiting, tapping her fingers on the table impatiently. She was dressed in the same black outfit as yesterday, her short, highlighted hair pulled back into a layered ponytail. She was pretty, and it was intimidating, but Therin had no time for being intimidated. She was going to intimidate her.

Taking a breath, Therin uttered a greeting, "Up already?"

Sira sighed, "I was hoping someone here might finally have some answers."

"Riiiight. Well, they sorta assigned the wrong person to you. Since the last recruit will be arriving today, we'll probably have a meeting or something to talk about the… thing… that Anima wants us to do. Did you meet Anima?"

She rolled her eyes. Never mind, Therin was starting to like her, "Yeah, only after she summoned me ten thousand feet up."

And the tension was broken. Therin felt that she could laugh, which, of course, she did, "Don't worry, you're not the only one who's a little peeved at her methods."

"A little? Yeah, now I'll never get my homework done. You say time runs the same here as it does in the real world?"

Questions, the bane of her existence. Nonetheless, Therin did her best to give an intelligent answer, "Yeah." She was kinda hurried.

"And, if this is Dream, which is literally the world of sleep, how come we still need to sleep?"

Again, she pondered long and hard on her response, "I dunno."

Sira muttered something under her breath. Therin figured she probably didn't want to know what it was. The noob spoke aloud to her, though, "Fine, teach me how to use magic."

Therin paused for effect, "Well, actually, it's called Essence, and each of us recruits has a large amount of it. And all of the indigenous inhabitants of Dream-"

"I don't care, just teach me before we get into exposition or whatever. That's always boring in a book."

Therin sighed again, "All right, no need to be contrary. The easiest way for me to learn was to connect to something I already loved. I always feel tranquil watching a fire. Not exactly safe, as everyone keeps telling me, but I have it under control. Y'know, now, anyway."

"Not sure I wanna hear the story." Sira thought for a moment, "I always love the sound of water."

Of course. She probably wanted to skip through the tulips as well. But whatever, "Follow, me, then; there's a bridge that goes over a river near here."

Not wanting to wait, Therin practically leaped for the door, eager to be out in the fresh air again. The recruits' dorms were in a courtyard, adjacent to a couple of small businesses, such as a bakery, a weapon smith (Therin always liked how cool the weapons turned out), and a florist, because friendliness. And flowers in Dream tended to be... murderous. They were kind of dangerous when you didn't know what you were doing, but point them at the monster and promise the bouquet pellets afterward and that's one job done.

The courtyard was made of obsidian, smooth and dark purple, which was a weird choice, considering how bright the rest of Daydream was. But whatever; it supported her feet well. Oh, yeah, Therin never wore shoes. When you can heal any injury, what's a little rawness?

Across the courtyard, the open space narrowed into a street lined with houses and stores. A little further and after a right turn, a series of bridges carried the street over the rough river crisscrossing the city. That's where they were headed.

The morning was early, so the sky, a rich indigo, was sporting a few scattered morning stars, but in the east, it faded to a brighter pink, indicating a late dawn. A few Dreamers (people who lived in Dream) were out and about doing their business; opening their shops, watering box gardens, and the like. Therin waved hello to an elf named Gerome. He tended to stay indoors all day playing video games in his mom's basement, so it was a rare sight to see him actually going as far as his mailbox.

Glancing back, she saw Sira trailing behind her, looking around in mild awe. When she had arrived in Daydream, it had been late at night, so Therin guessed that the poor girl hadn't been able to take much in before collapsing in the bed she was guided to.

Rounding the intersection, Therin spotted the first bridge ahead. This one was the largest, but it was a simple cobblestone construction with a thick support in the middle of the water, which rushed by in a swift froth today. She could hear the roar from where she was, and it sounded particularly furious, even more so than normal. But, if Sira liked water, this was the best and nearest place for her to connect with it.

As they strolled closer to it, Sira seemed to focus more on the river than on anything else around it. She began running ahead of Therin. She was surprised, since Sira had gone from in awe to totally focused within seconds; a full one-eighty. Therin jogged to catch up, watching Sira lean over the wall of the bridge, apparently fascinated with the white water below. Her eyes were closed, as if hearing it were all she needed. Strange girl. Then again, Therin, when she was five, liked climbing high trees and poking at fires, so who was she to judge.

She leaned against the wall of the bridge confidently, also listening to the current that could potentially kill her if she fell in. After a few seconds, Therin grew bored and decided to get on with the "lesson", "So, if you're ready, just imagine a link between you and the water."

Sira looked over, suspicious, "That's it? No clearing my mind or meditation or anything like that?"

Therin shrugged, "I've been told the matter here is very pliable, whatever that means. I just like to think of it as friendly, unlike some people I know."

She rolled her eyes again, "I hope you don't mean me?"

"Just a warning. Now, focus on doing something with it."

"Such infinite wisdom."

Therin took her turn rolling her eyes, "Just do it; the sooner you establish a link with one thing," she added a dramatic flair, "the sooner the wide world will be opened to you."

Sira took the advice to heart and once again narrowed her focus on the water. Finally. She reached out her hands, obviously trying to manipulate it in an easier way.

Somewhat curious, Therin turned over and leaned on her elbows. It occurred to her that she hadn't done anything to her hair this morning, so it was probably a mess. Quickly, she ran her hands over it. She could feel a few tufts out of place, but it was an easy fix. Concentrating just a little, she pulled a trickle from the water and ran it over her asymmetrical hairdo, the right side shaved short and the left shoulder length. She also had wolf ears on either side of her head, gray and white, which needed just as much grooming. Wolves were Therin's favorite animal, so even if people thought she was a furry, she wanted to wear the ears. They also had their uses, so they weren't all for show.

Pulling the extent of the water over her head, Therin managed to straighten her hair out, tangles and all. Her ears twitched, shaking the moisture off of themselves. Dropping the water back in, she turned to Sira, who had conveniently missed the whole thing.

Therin turned back to the river. A sizable bulge of stabilized, clear water had formed on the surface and was slowly separating itself from the body of water. Sira was sweating with the effort, but, eyes open, she was fierce, seeming to forcefully pull it out. Therin scolded herself. She was definitely a horrible teacher.

After a few more minutes of near fruitless efforts, Sira breathed deeply and let the bulge drop back in. She was clearly exhausted. Therin tried to think of how she interacted with matter. Thinking on the subject, she decided to relay her thoughts to her, um, student, "I usually think of myself as a guide for the matter, just telling it where to go and trust that it'll obey me, which, usually, it does."

"So there is a trick to it. Here I thought all magic techniques were the same." Sira voiced, sounding a little irritated.

"Have you studied this sort of thing?" Therin was actually curious; was there another kind of magic in the world - in the real world that she didn't know about?

Nodding, she responded, "Yeah. In order to write about certain things, I need to get a feel for what I like about different aspects of a few novels and make something new out of it."

Therin decided to embrace the change in subject and continued, "So you write. Like books, or just short stories?"

"Kind of."

Well, that really turned off the sudden conversation. And considering Therin had posed an either/or question rather than a yes or no, that left her confused as to what the response meant.

But, focusing on the lesson once more, she came full circle and tried a little something new to her, sincerity, "So, try one more time, but give the water a pathway upward, telling it to travel on it."

"Kay."

Sira closed her eyes again, this time more peacefully. She raised her hands again, waving them in a shape akin to a cylinder. No doubt that's what would form.

Sure enough, Therin observed ripples in the air directly above the river. Water, at first a small trickle, but gradually growing into a torrent, filled a circular tube of air, ascending into the sky. Below, the water level dipped, no doubt compensating for the large fountain Sira was constructing. The tube reached high and at the top, the water arched into a mist and slowly began to fall.

The mist was incredibly thick and soon, Therin could hardly see. Not only that, she was drenched. She set her palm alight, hoping to use the flame to burn away the cloud. She expanded the heat in order to dry her body and clothing as well.

When the cloud cleared, Sira was standing there, also soaked and, in addition, breathing heavily. Her disposition had changed dramatically, however, and she seemed elated, "I did it. I actually did it."

"Yeah, you did. Any other deductions, Sherlock?"

"Do you have to be so abrasive?"

Therin endorsed the banter, "Can I have a definition, judge?"

"That'll be deducted from your final score."

She shrugged, "I'm pretty sure that's not how spelling bees worked."

Sira shrugged back, "I never competed in one, so I don't know either."

"Yeah, whatever."

Once again enjoying the peacefulness of the scene, Therin leaned against the wall, looking across at the rest of the city. The sky had grown brighter fast. It looked like it was almost mid-morning, which meant the new arrival would be getting here soon. And then they could finally get moving out of this stinking city.

A woman, who was probably a pixie, floated by with her pet seal on a leash. As if to prove her point; things around here made no sense. Then again, in a place called Dream, she'd probably encounter a few illogical things.

"Therin!"

Speak of the devil. Therin and Sira looked up together into the sky where the spritely voice had originated. Above them, Ryan was flying down, which he often did. He was a weird kid, which Therin always loved to say, considering he was older than her. By four minutes.

For some reason or another, he had conjured up fox ears that were now growing on top of his head. Therin always thought he had similar reasons to her, but she could never be sure. He had long hair for a boy which always bounced around his normal ears and face. Like Therin, he had a small nose and a near constant, yet subtle smile.

But now, his face was concerned as he descended onto the bridge. He was panting, like he had rushed over here from somewhere far, "Therin, it's the new kid."

That piqued her interest, "What about him? And what about Olivia?"

He calmed down enough to respond, "Olivia's fine, but something's wrong with him. He won't move and he keeps telling her something about Dream."

"Sounds like he got overwhelmed," she turned to her star pupil, of whom she was very proud, "Well, what d'you say, Sira, wanna come with to make sure he's fine?"

Sira shrugged, "Might as well meet him now; from the sound of things, we're gonna be good friends either way. That, or worst enemies."

"Sounds like a plan."

Winking at Ryan, who would certainly understand, Therin started building up Essence. She jumped to take off and the air around her pushed her up.

Sira, still on the ground, yelled up to them, "Hey, no fair; you haven't taught me how to fly yet!"

Therin giggled, "That's your next lesson! Do try to keep up!"

She and Ryan soared in the direction of Nightmare with Sira close behind, managing to hover fleetingly between quick strides.

"This is it, Ryan!" She was excited to finally be going somewhere.

"Yeah, last guy, last day in Daydream. An adventure at long last." He seemed wistful. How unlike him.

"But you know that something uber cliché is gonna happen, right?"

"It is Dream. I suppose clichés are part of what makes this world."

"Then let's find out." She soared ahead, pushing herself just to meet the new kid, excitement coursing through her veins in place of blood.

Chapter 4
Olivia

Great, Olivia had somehow managed to mess up escorting Kyo. Yeah, Ryan and Therin had showed up to help get him to the barracks, but Olivia still felt like she could have helped him more. Or something. Why did life have to be complicated?

They waited outside the room they had put Kyo in, all of them in a sort of anxious silence. After he had collapsed and started trembling, he was unresponsive to anything. So, with an effort of combined wind magic, they had taken him back to the dorms and Sira was sent with specific directions to the nearest healer in the city. Upon returning with the water nymph, Sira seemed to want to do something more to help, but nobody knew how.

And now, Olivia and the others, bar Dom, were seated around the table, unable to shake the fear for Kyo's health. She could hardly bear the silence for much longer, so she tried to start conversation, "So, you're Sira?"

The blonde girl looked over, sullen, "Yeah, what of it?"

"Have you been able to tap into your Essence, yet?"

Sira raised an eyebrow, "If you're trying to distract me from the situation, it's not working."

Therin, across the table from Olivia, groaned, obviously bored, "If we're going to wait, can we at least do something with our time?"

Ryan shook his head, "No, I'd rather be here when Kyo wakes up. That way, we can help him out with his confusion."

Olivia agreed, "Yeah, and I bet, considering where I rescued him from, he's probably more confused and afraid than any of us probably were."

Sira piped up, "Where did you rescue him from, again?"

"A forest called Nightmare. And as you have probably guessed, names in Dream are pretty straightforward."

"But not anything in Dream." She speculated.

"Correct," spoke a voice from the doorway.

They all turned to see Dom, a tall, stocky kid. He was about fourteen, so, he was kind of imposing to the younger three recruits.

Regardless, he was really kind, but didn't always seem to feel comfortable around the others, which is why, whenever they planned in the morning, he chose things to do that would leave him solitary. Olivia could never figure out why this was, but she figured it was better to let him do his own thing.

As of now, he was wearing a brown leather jacket, a red beanie, a red shirt, and some loose-fitting jeans. Brown hair, green eyes, pleasant facial features, blah, blah, blah. Now Olivia could get back to listening rather than describe him.

"Since this world is called Dream, what do you think that implies?" He asked.

Sira responded, initiating the conversation, "One of two things, that it is either made up of our dreams, or it is what makes up our dreams."

"You are right on both accounts, but that's not what's important. What *is* important is how is Kyo?"

As if to answer his question, the door opened, revealing the water nymph, a kind lady who went by Niomi, "He should be up and about in a couple minutes. I wasn't able to restore his full memory, but he has remembered some things that he wants to talk to you about."

Olivia tilted her head to the side, "How did you communicate with him? He can't speak naturally."

"I know sign language." And Niomi took her leave, melting into a puddle and seeping through the stone.

Dom rolled his eyes, "I wish she wouldn't do that; it raises our rent by a ton when the inspectors see the damage."

Therin seemed excited, "More to the point, we finally get to do something! Come on, let's go talk to him."

They all filtered in, but Olivia held back. How come he hadn't spoken to her yet? She had established the telepathic link and it could span more than a little distance, as she was able to send a message to Dom and Ryan. Perhaps he wanted to keep his thoughts private. Or maybe he was too stressed. Whatever the case was, Olivia hoped she could fix it.

Are you coming? I can't speak to anyone else.

She breathed a sigh of relief; she had gotten worried over nothing, so Kyo was okay and her magic was still working. *Yeah, just a little hesitant.*

Hurry, please. She found his mental voice strange, but cute, like a child that was doing an impression of someone much older than them.

She entered the room and Kyo's fierce black eyes fixed on her. His face was expressionless, but his eyes… they rang out in pain. He seemed to be communicating more with them than with his telepathy.

The others were gathered closely around him, with Therin and Ryan sitting on either side of his bed and Dom and Sira standing next to them. They were watching Olivia as she entered. Therin, clearly impatient, spoke, "Well? When are you gonna let us speak to him? None of us understands sign language and you're the only one who can unlock telepathy."

She smiled, "Don't worry, I'll get right on it." Olivia told them to gather around Kyo. She linked each of their thoughts and his in turn by touching both of their heads at once, imagining a communication line reaching between her fingers and connecting them.

Eventually, all of them were linked to Kyo, and they proceeded to test their newfound connection, *I'm Therin!*

And I'm Ryan.

Sira.

Dom.

"And since you know me already, I won't use italics, since it might become confusing. In fact, Kyo here should be the only one using italics except in emergencies." Olivia thought it was a good idea, since it would definitely be easier if only one person communicated through thoughts.

I was going to introduce myself, as well, but you all seem to know me pretty well already.

Sira was straight to the point, "You said you had something to tell us?"

Kyo hung his head, *Yeah, but it's not good. First of all, I have no memory. Or voice, apparently.*

Therin nodded, "Yeah, we got that. So, what do you have to say that's bad?"

Well, I… I live - or, I guess lived here in Dream.

Ryan seemed confused, "But if you're an inhabitant of Dream, how can you be a recruit?"

Dom shushed him, "The only limits to being a recruit was to have a strong Essence. There's nothing that says you have to be in a coma."

Therin sighed, "Who told you that? Anima?"

"Actually, yeah."

"Oh."

Looking at him, Olivia couldn't believe it; he looked so normal, so much like a human. And there was nobody in Dream that she had heard of that had any similar sort of disability. She simply had assumed that he had been human. But now that they knew he was an inhabitant, that could mean anything.

Sira interrupted her thoughts, "Well, let's not dwell on it. If it yields useful information later, that's great, but for now, I know nothing, so it would be nice to have some answers."

Kyo nodded, his wavy black hair glistening, *I can get behind that. Like, for example, who's Anima?*

Dom stepped in, "Anima's a higher being who oversees Dream, though she can interfere only so often. You'll probably never meet her. Supposedly, she has a counterpart name Animus, but I've never met him. And I'm not sure I want to."

Olivia had never heard of Animus, but it seemed logical. And knowing Dom, he had probably gotten the information from study in the library in Daydream, since that's where he spent his time whenever he wasn't performing duties for the city.

"Eh, who cares about that? Shall we move to the dining room to answer the rest of the questions?" Olivia suggested.

Therin protested, "Can we do it outside?"

She always wanted to do things outside. Dom asked for a vote and even Kyo, still in bed, agreed it was a good idea.

Several minutes later, they were sitting around a fire pit, a small flame just being started by Therin. Kyo, though he had had a hard time standing and walking at first, had made it out okay and was seeming to enjoy the fresh air.

Sira went right to the point again, "all right, now, what exactly is our Essence?"

Olivia didn't know how to answer, so she looked at Dom, "Would you care to explain? I was never one for studying."

"Fine." He consented, "So, think of Essence like a battery. Or perhaps renewable energy. It fuels certain objects to do certain things. In the inhabitants, it's their life force. For us, and for Kyo, as well, for some reason, who already have a life force, it enables us to have abilities greater than would be possible for even those who are born with Essence."

And what about the Reaper? Kyo was curled up, as if he were afraid to ask the question. Olivia could understand; for such a cliché name, it was really ominous. And Dream names never lied, so it definitely was scary.

Therin, satirical as always, responded, "The Reaper reaps. Don't ask me why."

Dom corrected her, "What she means is that it sucks the Essence out of everything it comes across. So far, it hasn't made a move towards here, but it's only a matter of time."

Ryan raised his hand timidly, "Yeah, um, about that…"

That was worrying; usually, Ryan talked a lot, but he had been quieter than usual today, so Olivia knew something was wrong, "You don't mean…?"

"Yeah," he choked out, "I saw it when I was scouting, a big dome of gray, just like you said. It's on its way here from the south. The Reaper also has a horde of demons with it."

"How far away did you see it?" She asked. It could already be too late to flee, but if there was a chance they could save Daydream…

"It wasn't too far from the marsh."

So it was really close. And too late as well.

Dom sighed, "That's all right, Ryan, we'll just have to cut our losses."

Sira looked shocked, "'Cut your losses'?! And just leave a whole city to be destroyed? Are you that callous?"

He shook his head, "That's not it, it's just that Anima told me that whatever the Reaper destroys will eventually be restored."

"Then why are we fighting it?"

It'll just grow stronger and stronger until the damage is permanent. Or until it envelopes all of Dream. Am I right? Kyo asked, still frozen in the fetal position.

Dom nodded.

Of course. Olivia had heard some of this before, but the rest was still new to her.

Sira kept going, "So how do we stop it, then, if we can't just let it go?"

Olivia knew the answer, and it wasn't good, "We don't know. It was the one thing Anima never told us, no matter how much we asked. We've come up with a few ideas, but nothing we can imagine working."

Dom added, "So our plan right now is to find someone who can help us with that, or find out on our own. Kyo, if anybody comes to mind?"

Yeah, but I'm not sure how much I'll be able to remember.

"It's all right, just don't hurt yourself."

Olivia looked at the sky, it was probably past noon. If Ryan had seen the Reaper at the marsh a few hours ago, they had just enough time to prepare if they wanted to leave before it actually got here. As for the army of demons... there was really no telling. "We should probably get ready to go."

Sira agreed, "Yeah, but I'm still not happy about it."

"It's hard to accept," Dom consoled, "but there's nothing we can do for them but stay alive. The Reaper will still kill us, too."

Therin poked the fire, which promptly singed the firewood to ashes, leaving the air around them sweltering, "Fine, let's get out of here."

Chapter 5
Ryan

Ryan was not happy. First of all, he had made friends in Daydream who he would miss. Second, he was the one who had been too afraid to speak. Third, they as a group were leaving the city to die voluntarily. Needless to say, he felt awful. And since he was the same age as Olivia, well, the older kids probably felt worse.

As he shouldered his pack and left his room, ready to leave, he thought about the situation. If the Reaper did attack Daydream, wasn't it possible it would eventually catch up to them, as well? What would they do then, if they were cornered by the army of demons that he saw?

Kyo came out of his room, also ready to leave. He saw Ryan and made eye contact with him, *It's okay to be scared.*

Yeah, but I feel awful just thinking about leaving Daydream unprotected. Ryan explained. It was true, no matter how many times they told him it was all right.

Look, even if you had said something earlier... I'm not sure how I know this, but I think Daydream would have been lost anyway.

How do you figure?

Kyo paused, as if phrasing his answer very carefully, *People can be stubborn sometimes.*

Therin came up behind Ryan and poked him, "Surprise! What are you two chattering about, your love lives?"

Kyo blushed and Ryan scoffed, "Like we could have any here. And besides, Kyo probably doesn't remember any girls."

"Fair enough, but I know you still like Aly."

Ryan was irritated, "Yeah, we were shipped, like, that one time, but that doesn't mean I like her."

Therin smiled, seemingly enjoying the banter, "And what about Olivia, huh? You guys spend a lot of time on missions together."

"I hope you don't mind, but back off. I've been through enough without you pestering me."

"Kyo seems to be enjoying it."

Ryan glanced over. Sure enough, though normally expressionless, the edgy mute was trying to cover a smile, though not very well, "Hey, who's side are you on?"

She's just trying to take your mind off of things. It's actually really nice of her.

Ryan blinked. He hadn't thought of it that way, but it was true, he really had been distracted for a moment there. Ryan was actually starting to appreciate his sister.

Therin frowned, walked right up to Kyo, and promptly pushed him, "Way to spoil it, Kyo. I just might have gotten him to 'fess up, but no, you had to go and tell him my ulterior motive."

They had a staring contest, Kyo's black eyes locked on her dark blue ones. Obviously, they were also holding a private argument, one to which Ryan wasn't invited. Eventually, Therin threw up her hands in defeat, "Fair enough, you win."

Sira, Dom, and Olivia simultaneously (more or less) walked into the room, Dom seeming particularly amused, "What's this all about?"

Nothing in particular.

Sira shrugged, "Fine, just wanted to know what all the yelling was about. Are we all ready to go?"

They all had a bag of sorts strapped to them. Therin was carrying less than everyone else, since she claimed she could grow her own food and shelter. Luckily, that meant no one else had to, but they had packed snacks for on the road as well.

Kyo began walking toward the door, *Come on, then.*

Dom rolled his eyes, "Tell me why we're letting the mute amnesiac who can't communicate with anyone else lead the way?"

Olivia shrugged, falling in line, "I guess he's just ready to leave."

Ryan looked at Kyo. Since he was much older than Ryan, it struck him as odd that he didn't behave more like Dom, or even that he hadn't quite shown any signs of Essence yet. Nevertheless, he seemed to exude the sort of air that Ryan looked up to. It felt odd to him, being able to look at someone and immediately wanting to be their friend.

Therin came up behind him and tugged on one of his fox ears, "Come on, stop staring. Let's go."

Ryan nodded, rubbing the top of his head. They had a lot to do.

Looking back, Ryan saw that there was no trail. At least, there wasn't a visible one. Any adversaries would most likely have a hard time tracking them. Most likely.

They were almost at the crest of the last hill before the Red Forest. Apparently, it wasn't a special enough place to have a sleep-oriented name. Once they passed over the hill, they would be completely out of sight of Daydream.

Walking was getting tedious; Ryan controlled the air currents around him, gliding up past the others, the rushed feeling taking his breath away temporarily. The fresh air filled his nostrils, clearing his mind and helping him to think straight. He reached the top and looked down at the others. Therin was close behind, also flying, Olivia was streaking along at a blinding speed, Dom was leaping high, Sira was fitfully gliding, still trying to master the art of flight. Kyo simply jogged, the incline slowing his progress.

Need some help? Ryan transmitted.

That would be nice, yes.

Ryan focused on the earth under Kyo. Causing it to ripple, he quickly pushed Kyo up the hill, who stumbled due to the rough acceleration. About halfway up, Kyo's face took on an intrigued expression. He closed his eyes, touched the ground, and it stopped. Ryan could feel resistance, so he pushed the earth harder, yet it still didn't move.

Kyo looked up at Ryan, *I think I got this.*

Reluctantly, he relinquished his grip on the soil. Immediately, Kyo surged up the hill with even more speed than Ryan had provided him. When he reached the top of the hill, a spire of earth launched Kyo into the sky. His descent slowed, and Ryan could feel the wind swirling around him. Kyo looked stunned, as if he had pulled off a trick he didn't think he could do, which he had, in a sense. Therin glided up to him, clearly impressed.

"Where in the world did you learn to do that? It's almost as if you've done it thousands of times!"

Kyo closed his eyes contemplatively, *I don't know. I just kind of felt Ryan's magic and played with it.*

"Well, that was certainly more impressive than anything I could do," Sira praised from nearby, out of breath.

Olivia seemed just as intrigued, "Perhaps you could do it again?"

Dom nodded, "Yeah. If you already know how to use your Essence, that would be an amazing thing to know."

I'll try.

Kyo squatted to the ground again. With a light touch, nothing happened. He put his hand more forcefully against the earth, straining enough that veins popped out on his skin. He pulled his hand up. A few pebbles followed it. *Sorry. I guess it was a lot harder this time.*

Dom shook his head, "No, even this is great; now we know your Essence, for whatever reason, just needs a little help to get going. We'll make sure to help you get stronger, don't worry."

Sira raised an eyebrow, "How come you're best friends already?"

He shrugged, "No idea. Maybe he's just the kind of person I can get along with?"

Therin called from above, since she had apparently gotten bored enough to fly, "Guys, you need to see this."

Ryan called up, "Not all of us can fly, you know. What's so cliché that we need to see it now?"

She touched down and pointed towards Daydream, "That."

They all turned in the direction she had indicated, apprehension hanging in the air. On the crest of one of the southern hills surrounding the city was a dome of gray, debris swirling around it. The edge of the grass adjacent to it was gray, the color having been sucked out of it. Looking through the arch of desaturation, the untouched territory was a negative image, the colors harsh and imposing.

Upon closer inspection, there was a swarm of living beings amassing near it and heading in their direction. Fast.

Dom spoke up, "Demons, no doubt."

Therin rolled her eyes, a special skill of hers, "Duh."

Definitely. Kyo agreed.

Ryan chimed in, "Den - I mean, then we should probably run, right?"

In response, the others took off, getting a head start on Ryan, "Nice to know you guys care so much."

Quickly catching up, Ryan addressed Dom, "Those demons are faster than us; how will we get away?"

Slowing his pace to match Ryan's, he suddenly looked concerned, "You're right. We could fly or increase our speed, but Sira and Kyo can't do that on their own. If we help them out, it might be too much strain on the rest of us."

"Any suggestions?"

Dom thought for a second more, "Catalyze Kyo, then maybe he can help us help Sira."

"I'll get on it," Ryan assured.

No need, Kyo thought, *I heard the whole thing. I'm sure I can help out with a little boost.*

Here's a little wind, then. Ryan conjured a channel of air directly at Kyo. The other boy reached out his hand toward the gust and made a motion as if pulling it around himself. His face became even more blank, as if he were now going into a reflexive action.

Ryan's fox ears twisted behind him, so now he was hearing in almost 360 degrees, a trick he rather enjoyed. He could hear the demon army gaining, their heavy footsteps or wing beats drumming in his head. Their excited chattering stabbed his mind. He angled his ears forward again.

Therin glided next to him, "A rowdy bunch, aren't they?"

"Yeah."

"Are you gonna fly anytime soon?"

Ryan huffed, refusing to answer verbally. Instead, he crouched to the ground and pulled a flat blade of rock to the surface. Hopping onto it, he smoothed the earth in front of him and conjured two jets of wind from his hands, pushing him along as if he were snowboarding.

He wove around small obstacles, using his hands when necessary. He was having a lot of fun with it, considering he was fleeing from a demon army. Ryan checked over his shoulder, but quickly regretted it. There were a couple of bat-like demons that were diving after him from the air. He spun, slicing into the dirt and launching blades of condensed soil at his assailants. All three targets crumpled to the ground, pierced by the rock in many places, dissolving quickly.

In the brief reprieve, Ryan drew the weapon he had, uh, borrowed from the city armory, a short, curved sword. He had found it was most easily wielded backhand, so he twisted it around so it protected his forearm.

Beside him, Olivia ran, her pace impossibly fast, "Having fun?"

He scrunched up his face, "Not really, you?"

"Yeah, loads of fun. Can't wait to fight for my life."

Sira, practically being dragged by Dom and Kyo through the air, looked positively grumpy, "At least you're not having to rely on others."

Therin, tailing behind, giggled, "Just use the water in the air!"

"I'll help you get started," Dom offered, even though he clearly had his hands full.

Not stopping, Dom summoned a small platform of water and encased it in ice. He dropped Sira onto it and froze her feet to it. He started moving it, but his flight rapidly slowed with the divided concentration. Kyo swooped in, silent, but imposing. He motioned towards the ice and it lurched forward, matching his gliding pace. Sira took a hint and concentrated as well. Soon, Kyo relinquished the platform, but it continued moving forward.

Sira exclaimed, "Hey, I'm getting the hang of it!"

Ryan was impressed, but he risked another glance back, "Just in time, too."

While they had been working on mobility, another squadron of demons had come over the top of the hill. Apparently, their trail wasn't cleverly hidden. Two brutes like minotaurs charged down the terrain, their singular, large horns pointed menacingly at the six of them. Four black, leopard-shaped demons flanked the minotaurs. They all had elegant spikes bristling on their entire bodies.

From the air, a large demon, which looked like a cross between an eagle and a vegetable, screeched down at them, shooting spines from its lumpy neck. Most of the spines, nearly invisible, were directed at Dom, who swerved, desperately avoiding the darts. The grass where the spines landed morphed into another veget-eagle, this one smaller and covered with downy feathers.

One of the leopards leaped over Ryan and landed in a defensive crouch, its spines expanding like a blowfish. In the narrow space allowed, he slid under the beast, his sword curved towards its stomach. The spikes, surprisingly tough, resisted Ryan's blade. He cleared the beast, which immediately depuffed and began chasing him again.

Out of nowhere, Olivia flashed into existence, directly in between Ryan and the beast. She reached out and held it firm by its uncovered nose. All it had to do was open its mouth and it could devour her. Instead, it turned and jumped at one of the minotaurs. Satisfied, Olivia streaked away again.

Sira, applying herself to the combat, twirled her platform, shards of the ice separating themselves and launching at the enemy. Several shards found their mark in one of the bad leopards, instantly dissolving it. Dom intercepted the veget-eagle at close range, slicing off its wings with a jagged sword. Lightning arched from the sword to the eagle and vaporized it in midair. Back on the ground, Therin danced around a minotaur, leaving roaring flames in her wake. The poor beast was confined as it slowly burnt to death, bellowing in agony. Therin simply laughed.

Kyo, somewhat glowing now, approached one of the remaining leopards. It reflexively puffed up at his approach, but Kyo didn't slow down. In an instant, he disappeared, as if he were never there at all. The leopard, clearly confused, allowed its guard to drop. Moments later, Kyo appeared behind it and twisted his hands as if wringing out a rag. The leopard contorted in response, the front of back halves ripped apart brutally. Ryan could barely stand to watch as the demon evaporated.

There was only one bad leopard left, which Ryan decided to tackle. He rushed at it, and it seemed to smile in response. It puffed up and Ryan stopped in his tracks. Concentrating, he forced two pillars of earth on opposite sides of the beast, crushing its spines and wedging it in place. Ryan jumped and flipped, his blade spinning on the outside of his acrobatics. It slashed into the beast, which promptly dissolved into shadow.

He looked around. The others were all right and unscathed. The leopard that Olivia had inexplicably tamed was with her beside the slowly dissolving corpse of the other minotaur. Everyone else was gathering around Kyo, apparently. Ryan jogged over to join them.

Kyo was on the ground, convulsing slightly. His eyes were closed and he wasn't glowing anymore. In fact, his skin looked white, almost turning gray.

Ryan gasped, "Is he gonna be okay?"

Dom examined him, "He looks bad. I think he'll recover, but he's in no shape to travel. We won't be getting away from the army."

"Didn't we beat the ones who knew about us, though?" Sira asked.

Olivia shook her head, "No, those were probably the scouts. When they don't return, the rest of the army will know where to look. They're actually pretty smart, for a bunch of globs of darkness."

"Yeah, and we'll likely be overwhelmed if we have to fight them all at once."

Worried now, Ryan asked, "So how do we escape?"

Hide... It was Kyo. He had stilled, but his skin hadn't changed and his eyes remained closed.

Sira looked at the others, "Can we do that?"

Dom and Olivia looked at each other, obviously conversing silently. Therin whispered in Ryan's ear, "I hate when they do that."

He whispered back, "They have been here the longest."

"Fair point."

In unison, Olivia and Dom raised their hands. A pearly dome arose from the dirt, encompassing both the party and their new pet. Once it closed off at the top, it became nearly invisible to them, a milky sphere encircling them.

"It's a camouflage sphere," Dom explained, "It'll mask our scent and our sight, but it won't do anything for our sound. If any demons come this way, it'll turn their attention away. If the Reaper comes... well, we'll cross that bridge when we come to it."

Ryan sat down. Opening his pack, he dug out a couple of snacks.

Therin sat down in front of him, "Can I have some?" Ryan shushed her, but the only thing she did was lower her volume, "Ah, come on; I'm your sister, so you have to share."

"Grow your own."

"But I can't grow chocolate."

"Guys," Dom interrupted, "I'm serious about silence. Therin, if you're hungry, you can grow your own food, like you said would. Just nothing crunchy."

She rolled her eyes, but said nothing in response. Instead, she stood up and moved to sit by Kyo, who was slowly looking better.

Behind him, Olivia tapped Ryan on the shoulder. He looked at her and saw that she was pointing down the hill. Right at the bottom, a troop of demons was coming around the lip where the hill met the flat ground. They weren't many, but enough to miss if they disappeared.

As they climbed the hill, Ryan could see that they were looking around for something, presumably the recruits. The demons reached a point level with the camouflage. One looked right through Ryan, but immediately stared ahead once more.

Collectively, they held their breath as the demons passed. One stooped, probably trying to catch a scent. When it started walking in circles trying to pinpoint one, it gave up and rejoined its comrades. Once they were all out of sight, Ryan allowed himself to breath.

"I wasn't sure it would work for a moment there," Sira sighed.

Seemingly offended, Olivia responded, "Thanks for the vote of confidence."

Dom interrupted, "Whatever the case, we're not out of the woods yet. I think we should lie low until tonight, try to get some sleep and get moving under cover of darkness."

Therin waved him off, "All righty, cliché master. Next thing you know, we'll be running out of rations and be stranded in the middle of the desert, but whatever. G'night everyone!"

Therin immediately fell asleep, not even rolling out her sleeping bag before collapsing on it. Following her rather abrupt example, Ryan more carefully set up his sleeping area. After a little adjusting, he finally settled down and, despite the sun low in the sky, began to dream within Dream.

Chapter 6
Dom

    Dom honestly had no idea how he had gotten to the point in his life where he could say that he was hiding from demons in a rudimentary invisibility cloak. He had also simultaneously dragged someone in ice and evaded a flying squash. In hindsight, it was a funny story to tell the grandkids, but he had been terrified in the moment. The story of his life. But now Dom was here, in a point of his life where such things were commonplace. He had seen crazier things, even, but it still scared him how normal it seemed.
    Looking up at the sky, Dom guessed it was probably about seven o'clock, based on the twilight. No other demons had come this way, but Dom was still having a hard time sleeping. If the reaper still had a possibility of being in the area, there was reason to fear, which Dom preyed upon, using it to fuel his energy to keep watch. The on-the-job training he had given Sira had exhausted him, so now he was struggling to stay awake.
    Not only was he looking out for the group in general, but he was also concerned about Kyo, who had only gained a little of his healthy complexion back, so he was still pale. If Dom didn't know any better, he would say that Kyo was asleep, but, judging from the fact that he had spoken to all of them earlier, he was most likely awake, but struggling from an extreme agony, one that encompassed his consciousness.
    Wow, that was depressing. If Dom thought like that, no wonder narrating came easily to him. And yet, he still had trouble reading between the lines. It was odd, but he had learned to live with it.
    He heard rustling next to him and turned his head to see Olivia, who met his eyes with concern, "How're you holding up?"
    "Fine. Nothing's wrong."
    She leaned her head to one side, "You don't have to pretend with me. You forget; I've been here a lot longer than the others, so I know when something's bothering you."
    Sighing, Dom responded, "Fine, you caught me," He gestured to Kyo, "I made a new friend."

"And now he's fainted."

"Actually, I think he's still awake."

"Huh." Olivia leaned over and touched Kyo's forehead, almost immediately pulling back, "Um, ow."

Dom knew what that meant. So his suspicions were correct, "That bad?"

She nodded, rubbing her arm absentmindedly. Her leopard plodded up to her and nuzzled her lightly.

He looked up at the few evening stars, feeling the silence more than anything. There was an edge to it, like the world holding its breath before a tornado touches down. Or when a star athlete gets carried away unmoving on a stretcher.

Olivia tapped his shoulder and her hand moved into his line of sight, pointing up the hill. Lots of pointing today. Dom glanced up and nearly had a heart attack.

The dome of gray, the Reaper, was crawling over the hill, turning the plants ashen.

Dom immediately stood up, *Help me wake everyone.*

What about Kyo?

If it gets close enough and we have to run, we'll carry him.

Unsure of whether or not the Reaper could respond to sound, Dom and Olivia silently woke the others up, careful to cover their mouths as they awoke. Sira and Dom crouched on either end of Kyo, ready to pick him up at a moment's notice. There were no demons around and the camouflage was still in place, so hopefully, they could go without being noticed just this once. Great, he probably just jinxed it.

As the Reaper inched its way past the dome, within an arm's reach of the border, Dom once again held his breath. The widest part of it came within millimeters of their sanctuary and he swore he could hear the Essence being sucked out of the ground beneath the dome. This close, he was able to see in greater detail what was inside it. A smaller, darker dome, ominously black, was pressing against the border of the Reaper, apparently steering it. It was attached by a cord to a spot in the center. It looked no different from the rest of the Reaper besides a ring around it. Dom was clueless as to what it was for.

Just as he thought they were safe, a growl escaped from the leopard's throat. Immediately, the darker dome swiveled in their direction, pushing the Reaper at the group. Dom and Sira simultaneously lifted Kyo, who weighed virtually nothing between them. They all ran in the same direction, but not directly away from the Reaper.

As soon as the two domes collided, the milky, protective one shattered and Dom felt exposed. Feelings of fear and hopelessness overcame him. He knew it was the Reaper trying to manipulate him, so he stubbornly pushed through it, hoping the others could do the same. At the bottom of the hill, a line of trees, the Red Forest, stood tall, seeming impervious to the group, for maneuvering would be awkward for Sira and Dom, considering how unwieldy a human body was.

Olivia and her leopard came astride with the two of them, a rudimentary saddle strapped onto its back. She ushered the Sira and Dom to put Kyo onto it. When they did, he was strapped in. As long as the spines never extended, Kyo would be fine. Free of his cargo, Dom was able to run unhindered, with Sira close behind.

Nearing the tree line, Olivia and Therin forged ahead to clear a path, while the others trailed behind, staying by the leopard. Upon reaching the trees, the tame demon was swarmed by others of its kind who had been lying in wait. Dom fought hard to protect it while still progressing onward.

Using his jagged sword, he cut down and vaporized demon after demon, falling into a frenzied state. He cleaved through his foes with much more ferocity and recklessness than he usually allowed himself. The attackers gradually grew less frequent and soon were quelled entirely. They pressed onward, each taking a different path. Ryan and Dom guarded Kyo, while Sira skipped above the canopy, leaping from one platform of ice to another. Therin and Olivia were working tirelessly to maintain a good path by cutting or moving undergrowth.

Looking over his shoulder, Dom saw the Reaper still in pursuit, the hidden shapes within it now obscured. It wasn't gaining, but it also wasn't falling behind. And it was hungrily swallowing all that crossed its heedless boundary.

Needing no more motivation, Dom accelerated, knowing they were almost through the thinnest part of the forest. Ahead of them, another hill loomed, this one being the one Sira had described.

Not caring any longer for noise, Dom yelled over at Ryan, "Do you think we can push through the hill? It would be a lot faster than going over it."

Ryan, looking unsure, nodded, "Yeah, but I'll need help."

"You'll get it," He assured the kid.

Ahead, he transmitted to Olivia, *We're going to push through the hill, think you can help.*

I can try.

Satisfied, Dom started building up his Essence. Focusing on the earth around and in front of him, he imagined it bending at his touch, forming a sturdy tunnel through the hill. Simultaneously, Olivia, Therin, Dom, and Ryan all slapped the ground at the base of the hill and the tunnel began eating itself away, the walls, ceiling, and floor all hardened to be traversable.

The leopard, who seemed skeptical at first, went inside after being ushered by Olivia. Sira dropped into the tunnel and the others filed in behind her. The air inside was damp and heavy, so Dom had a little trouble breathing, the scent thickly masking his other senses.

Therin was ahead of Dom when she looked back, "Don't you dare take a look."

Dom heard rumbling. He didn't want to.

Due to their rapid progression, they soon cleared the tunnel. Without even a pause, Sira waved her hands over the water, which formed a raft out of ice. All of them piled in, except for the leopard, which swam alongside them. Sira and Therin worked together to bend the currents in favor of the raft, pushing it towards the edge of the plateau.

Now that they were out of the tunnel, Dom turned around, hoping to see the Reaper far behind. Unfortunately, it was right on their tail, no less than a few meters behind. He really hated himself for looking. The lake wasn't large, but it still took them several minutes to cross going at full speed. It didn't help that the Reaper went unchallenged by the liquid surface it was traversing.

Eventually, they ran aground and they quickly disembarked. Now the Reaper was gaining, and fast, as if it were desperate to reach them in this last stretch of ground. They sprinted for the cliff, just as eager to reach the end.

The leopard, weighed down by both Kyo and water, tripped and couldn't get back up. Olivia and Dom stopped, ushering the others to go on.

Olivia stroked the snout of the beast affectionately, "Her shoulder is dislocated. We'll have to untie Kyo and carry him."

Dom looked up at the Reaper, which had already reached the shore, "I don't think we have time."

"I can't leave them!"

Untie me.

Dom stared at Kyo, who stared back, his black eyes clear as the night sky. He shook his head, "But you're in no condition-"

Untie me!

Not wanting to argue, Dom did as he was told. Immediately, Kyo jumped up and, instead of running away from the Reaper, he leaped toward the dome and thrust out his hand to meet it. When the Reaper touched it, it halted and the air became stagnant. A horrible screeching rang through the air and it slowly began to retreat.

Go, I'll catch up. Don't argue.

Dom lifted the leopard onto his shoulders and pulled Olivia up. Together, they ran for the edge, preparing to jump. Dom glanced behind them and saw Kyo still holding up his hand, slowly backing away from the Reaper. When it tried to go around him, he altered his retreat to keep himself between it and the others. Dom returned his attention forward.

Ahead of them, Sira and Ryan had already jumped, but Therin was waiting for them, "Is Kyo gonna be all right?"

Dom hesitated, "Um…"

In response, Kyo broke his stalemate with the Reaper and began sprinting for them, his eyes glowing brightly, *Jump!*

Together, the three of them leapt off of the cliff, the wind boosting them away and slowing their descent. Moments later, Kyo also dived off, falling masterfully headfirst. Inexplicably, wings sprouted from his back and carried him softly to the ground. Dom, Olivia, and Therin soon joined him, Sira, and Ryan on the ground, aghast.

The wings winked out of existence, leaving no trace. Dom couldn't help but stare at him; for a guy that had been incapacitated moments ago, he hadn't done too badly. "Uh, how in the world did you do that? That's even more impressive than before!" Dom was thoroughly flabbergasted; as far as he knew, no one had ever resisted the Reaper before.

Ryan tugged on his sleeve, "Isn't that still gonna come after us?" He asked, pointing at the Reaper, which was stranded at the top of the sheer, rocky drop.

Dom shook his head, "No, it'll have to go around a couple miles until it reaches a slightly more agreeable slope. More importantly, Kyo, where did that come from?"

The mute shrugged, obviously as confused as everyone else, *No idea; one moment I couldn't move and the next, I was feeling strongly that I had to push against it.*

Therin shook her head, mouth agape, "But you fought the Reaper, nothing else can do that. Maybe that's what Anima had planned."

Olivia, who was tending to her leopard, chimed in, "Who knows with Anima? Maybe she knew and maybe she didn't. Whatever the case, we still need to find out how to actually beat it."

Sira nodded, "Yeah, but at least we know we have some protection against it. Where do we go now, Dom?"

"We're going to a city called Enrem. I've heard there's some kind of all-knowing entity there, even more so than Anima."

Ryan tapped his chin, "Enrem. Is that sleep related, perhaps?"

Sira raised her hand, "I'm guessing it's derived from NREM sleep."

Dom nodded. He looked up at the Reaper, which was wasting no time going north, the closest way to get to them.

Kyo shouldered his bag, *Guess we better get going.*

Dom turned and gestured for the rest to follow them, "Yeah, good idea."

Ahead of them, the moon was rising, half hidden by the line of mountains that they had to cross. Behind them, a raging, Essence sucking entity prepared to siphon out their souls. They chose the obvious route, though Dom was trying to ignore the fact that this vast world could have any number of trials in store for them.

Chapter 7
Kyo

Of all the things Kyo thought he would be able to do, stopping the Reaper in its tracks was not one of them. He had felt himself get stronger the closer he got to it, as if he was only strong when he needed to be. With his luck, that was true, and he would only be able to use his Essence to fight. After all, he hadn't needed a catalyst from any of the others to repel the dome of gray. But with no memory other than living in Daydream and his name, Kyo was clueless as to why this was. Stupid plot device.

Now, as the moon rose high and their arduous hike continued, Kyo was on edge. Already, they had been ambushed by demons and chased by an all-powerful Essence-taking thing, but they had overcome those, to a degree. So why was he scared? Maybe he was just tense in case it happened again.

He plodded along next to Therin, who seemed to be shadowing him. He continuously caught her taking sideways glances at him.

What is it? He demanded.

Her expression tightened, *I guess I'm just in awe; after looking around for some way to fight the Reaper, you just drop out of the sky.*

Sira fell out of the sky more than I did.

Therin quietly laughed, *Yeah, I guess you're right. But whatever, you're still super cool.*

Coming from someone that had lived and breathed Dream for as long as Therin had, Kyo took that as a huge compliment. He sighed, *That makes one of us.*

Therin shook her head slightly, *Five, actually. Maybe six, depending on what that leopard thinks.*

How are you so sure?

Just that you're so down about it; seriously, if you saved the world, I think you'd have to take antidepressants.

Kyo didn't respond. The only reason Therin could find humor in it was because it was true; he didn't know anything about himself, so this power confused him.

You still there?

Kyo exhaled forcefully, *Yeah, I don't really have any choice but to talk to you.*

Smiling, she replied, *Well, who else is gonna get you to look at everyone?*

What? He looked up, not realizing he had been staring at the ground for the entire silent conversation. The others, who had fallen back in line with Kyo, were all looking at him, intrigued.

"Having a private conversation?" Ryan teased.

Sira crossed her arms, "No shame in sharing any secrets."

Kyo could feel his face heating up, *It's not like that, we were just talking.*

"Suuuure."

Dom cleared his throat, "Come on, guys, leave him alone; we've all been through a lot tonight and we still have a lot of ground to cover."

Olivia, smiling, replied, "Sure thing, boss."

"I'm not the boss any more than you are."

And with that, they fell into silent trudging once more.

After walking for only forever, with the moon lowering itself and everyone almost nodding off, they reached the edge of another forest, this one more filled out than the Red Forest. There was a lot of crimson undergrowth, all of it seemed parallel to some form of plant life one might find in a real forest.

They decided to push through a little farther until they could find a decent place to make camp. Kyo, despite how difficult it was, kept his eyes open for such a place as Therin convinced the most obstructive bushes and such to stand aside for them.

Eventually, they stumbled upon a relatively open spot that was close to a river. The water ran west, away from the mountains. Pulling out their sleeping bags, they settled in while Therin and Ryan built a fire from fallen branches and leaves. Ryan formed a pit to keep it from spreading too far and Therin sparked the flame.

With Olivia and her leopard standing guard first, Kyo felt safe enough to fall asleep, staring up into the stars through the leafy trees. Thinking back on the day, it had all moved so fast; from where he had woken up to where he was now falling asleep, the distance was enormous. Thinking over all the memories he had made that day, he drifted into dreams.

He thought it was impossible, but Kyo knew he was dreaming. In Dream. He expected to see a spinning top, but he had no idea why. He was in a large room, furnished exquisitely with expensive looking tables, chairs, and shelves that were all carved to replicate scenes of various types, from happy to sad to scary. It made him feel uncomfortable and he ran out of the room through the ornate doorway.

Now he was outside, in the middle of the courtyard, which was bustling with people. One, a man with drooping ears and cheeks, gasped when he saw Kyo, pointed and appeared to yell something, but he couldn't hear what it was. The people around the man looked and exhibited a similar reaction and so on, until the entire crowd stood gaping.

One by one, they all began to kneel, their eyes looking expectantly and fearfully at Kyo. He couldn't move, couldn't ask them why they did so, only watch as five individuals, so shell-shocked they had not bowed, stood out from everyone else. Kyo inexplicably felt anger at their insolence. How dare they not submit to him! He could feel a hand of his rise to throw a bolt at the ne'er do wells.

With shock, he realized that they were his friends, Therin, Olivia, Dom, Sira, and Ryan, but he couldn't stop himself and both he and the others watched in horror as a glowing stream arched from them to his hand.

The dream jumped into another place, a void, black except for a squirming animal in front of him. It looked like some kind of worm, small and insignificant. Suddenly, a blade fell from above the worm, which split unevenly in half. The halves regenerated, one side larger than the other. Kyo closed his eyes; the scene, though simple, was too disturbing for him, as if he were the worm, waiting to be sliced in half.

Moments later, his eyes opened, looking up at the brightly lit leaves. It was probably about midday, but there was no way to tell with the canopy in the way. The fire had burned out, leaving dead coals and ash. Around him, everyone else was sleeping, including Olivia, who apparently hadn't awoken another watch. The only exception was the leopard, who sat with her head held high, her broken leg wrapped in a splint.

Ever since Kyo had learned she had a gender, and since Olivia had tamed her completely, he had learned to not be afraid of it. Even if she didn't have a name yet, she was still a loyal animal. As such, Kyo stood and nonchalantly walked over to the demon, unafraid of her striking out. The demon turned from her vigil to watch Kyo as he approached her.

When he sat next to her and looked out to the forest, Kyo saw her relax out of the corner of his eye. When her head was turned, he looked at her, eyes glancing over the sheen of the spines, each producing a pattern which, up close, was a lot more detailed than the pitch black that he had observed from afar.

Kyo looked back out at the rest of the camp. All of them were sound asleep, with the exception of Sira, who seemed to be tossing and turning. Perhaps he wasn't the only one who had dreams in Dream.

Regardless of whether he would dream or not, Kyo was reluctant to go back to his sleeping bag and fall back asleep. He was tired, but not terribly so, and he was okay with that.

He turned back to the leopard and tentatively reached out a hand. She seemed to sense his movement and her nose snapped around to sniff his fingertips. Once she deemed him harmless, she turned back to her watch. Kyo closed the distance and carefully set his hands on the spines. They were actually very dull and he began stroking them from her neck to her back. After continuing like this for a little while, the leopard began to purr softly.

"I wouldn't do that if I were you."

Kyo turned to see Olivia, awake and watching him. *Why not? She seems harmless.*

"Yeah, she does, but if you accidentally rub her the wrong way, the venom in those spikes will kill you within minutes."

He carefully retracted his hand from the leopard. Suddenly, she didn't seem so amiable, after all.

"Her name's Mia, by the way."

Mia. Such a normal name for a demon.

Olivia crawled over to Mia and scratched her snout, "She doesn't think of herself as a demon anymore; she's just a normal spike-covered leopard."

Kyo desired a change in subject, *What time do you think it is?*

"Time for you to get a watch. Let me check." Olivia got to her feet and leaped upward, easily phasing through the leaves.

He waited patiently, thinking about her comment about getting a watch. It was so smooth, as if that were her automatic response whenever someone asked that question. How amusing. She thumped back down onto the forest floor directly in front of him, "Judging by the sun, it's almost noon."

That's what I thought. Do you think we should get going?

"Yeah, and eat breakfast; I'm starving."

Kyo blinked, *But if we eat breakfast, then people will talk to me.*

"And I'm not talking to you?" Olivia seemed offended.

He looked out at the camp, *Well, you're not Therin.*

"Oh, I see, this is about Therin. Is she too happy for you? Or maybe, you're starting to like her?"

Seriously? I'm like, four, maybe five years older than her, depending on how old I am. Kyo was thankful there was no such thing as stuttering in telepathy.

"'Cause I can get her up if you want."

No, that's not-

"Okay, she's up." Olivia smiled, oblivious to Kyo's glare.

He looked over at Therin. Sure enough, she was up and walking over to meet them, stretching and yawning the whole way, "'Sup guys? What'd you need to talk about, Kyo?"

Olivia scratched Mia behind the ear, "I'll give you two some privacy."

When she was out of earshot, Therin asked, "What she on about?"

Kyo sighed; might as well tell her now, *She thinks I like you.*

She raised an eyebrow, another of her trademarks, *And do you?*

Great, now she was skeptical, too. Though, he felt the need to answer truthfully, even if he didn't know how. He thought back on the day before. He had talked to Therin a lot more than the others. He even enjoyed talking to her a bit, but he didn't have any romantic feelings for her, so he felt like they were just friends. Besides, since Kyo had no memory and Therin hadn't shared anything personal, it wasn't like they really knew anything about each other.

Well, I don't dislike you.

Therin smiled, *That's a start.*

He detected a tone that suggested she was hiding something, *What, do you like me?*

She giggled, *Not telling.*

Fair enough.

Olivia strolled over, "You guys don't mind if I interrupt?"

Therin punched her arm affectionately, "No, we just finished. What kind of jerk are you? He didn't know anything about his past!"

Kyo was taken aback; she had no reason to hide what they had been talking about, yet she had. He maintained a poker face.

Olivia looked at him, confused, "But I thought…"

That's my business, Olivia. How about you get everyone else up?

"I'll help!" Therin volunteered cheerfully.

Within minutes, everyone was up, the campsite had been stricken, and they had eaten a breakfast of oatmeal and fresh fruit.

Kyo looked at the river, and then at the mountains, *Y'know, if we follow the river, we might be able to find an easier place to get through the mountains.*

Dom responded, "How do you figure?"

Well, the river is coming from the mountains and looks relatively clean, so it must come from up there. If it doesn't, it might at least lead us to a point where we can cross through a valley.

Sira tapped her foot, "You may be right. Let's try it."

"As long as we get there soon. I'd love to sleep in a proper bed!" Ryan commented.

Therin nodded her agreement, her ear fur swishing.

Kyo looked ahead; the land next to the river wasn't as thick with undergrowth and there was even a small trail, as if wildlife often trod through here. It looked like the path would be easy, in the sense that they wouldn't have to push their way through plants. He started walking.

Chapter 8
Sira

Sira was walking next to Dom, who was helping her get the details straight, "Okay, so Anima is a higher being who assigned us to defeat the Reaper, which will eventually suck the Essence out of all of Dream. Essence is life force and magical power, depending on the holder, and it restores itself very slowly, so the Reaper will continuously get stronger. We have no idea of how to beat it, but Kyo, who apparently lived or lives in Dream is able to fight it somehow. And now, we're on our way to meet another powerful being who will tell us how to use Essence to fight an entity that eats Essence."

Dom nodded, "Sounds about right."

"Except," she added, "Olivia has some sort of taming ability that got us a leopard demon named Mia and telepathy is a normal form of communication here."

"There we go. Are you about up to speed?" Dom seemed genuinely concerned. How nice of him.

"I'm just having a hard time wrapping my head around this."

He smiled, "If it helps, don't think about all of it at once, just what you need to think about at the time."

Sira rolled her eyes, since that was the popular thing to do, "You make so much sense sometimes."

"Sometimes," his voice jumped higher in pitch for the first syllable, not like a voice crack, but a polished, practiced variance, and it was actually pretty funny, considering that Sira laughed briefly.

She stifled her laughter, "You certainly are a character."

"It would've been funnier if you had been there," he looked ahead, refusing eye contact.

Sira took that as a hint that he was thinking of before Dream. He would've been what, thirteen? "You miss it out there, huh?"

He turned back to her, a tear in the corner of his eye, "I've been in a coma for two years; how do you think my family feels? I know people have survived longer in comas, but… I'm worried they'll pull the plug on me."

Looking down at the ground, Sira was stunned into silence; she had no idea how to respond to his fear of death. Sure, they could die here, but they'd know if it happened. Dom, on the other hand, he had no idea from day to day if would die or not. Although, in a selfish sense, it made Sira feel happy that he could trust this sort of thing with her.

She looked in his eyes again; he seemed to be searching for her to say something, "Thanks for letting me know; that's gotta be a hard burden to carry. I think, technically, we're all in comas right now, if that makes you feel any better."

He sighed, "Sort of. And, if the rumors are true, Kyo isn't."

Again, Sira had no idea how to respond, since Dom had a way of twisting things into self-deprecation. They walked in silence together for a little while, not daring to break the ice.

Therin, who had been scouting ahead, trotted back with a grin on her face, "You're not gonna believe it, but there's a waterfall ahead!"

Ryan came up from behind her, breathing hard, "Yeah, it's awesome!"

Olivia came in line with them while riding on her leopard, showing no concern for the supposedly venomous spikes beneath her, "You hear that, Mia? Let's go look at the waterfall!" The demon-not-demon bolted off, going only half as fast as Olivia could go on her own.

Ryan and Therin turned on a dime and sprinted after her, calling, "Hey, wait!" etc.

Kyo walked up to watch the race, *Well, guess that just leaves the three of us.*

Dom smiled, "Race you?"

Holding up her hands, Sira feigned fear, "Woah, there, testosterone; remember, not all of us are super fit."

Go!

At Kyo's "shout", they took off, even Sira, thankful for the moment of frivolity. Within a minute or two of sprinting, she started slackening her pace, allowing the boys to forge ahead. When she caught up, they were on the ground, breathing heavily. She was about to scold them playfully, but her breath was taken away by the immense tower of water before her.

It cascaded over a rocky wall forty feet up. A sideways spire in the middle of it split the torrent in two, a gentler flow on one side, the other still heavy, crashing down forcefully into the pool below. The pool was small and immediately overflowed to form the river. The way it all went together so smoothly was what left Sira breathless, how such powerful forces of nature could come together into complete harmony.

Ryan and Therin were in the water, splashing each other with vigor, making sure the other got as wet as possible with each spray, indubitably using their Essences to their advantage. Olivia and her leopard were prowling along the side of the pool, strategically leaping in and splashing the others and leaping out before they received any retaliation. The whole scene was cute, innocent, even. And for a moment, bar the leopard, Sira could almost forget that they were in a fantastical world that was on the verge of collapse.

Dom, recovered from his physical exertion, started sizing up the cliff and the surrounding area. Sira didn't like his scrutinizing face, "Not good?"

He shook his head, "No; the rocks around the waterfall would be easier to climb, but they're wet, so it would be hard not to slip. And strangely enough, the walls that aren't wet are a lot smoother."

"Couldn't we just fly up?"

Slapping his forehead, Dom sighed, "Yeah, you're right. And you and Kyo?"

She thought a moment, "Well, there's enough water in the air for me to jump around on and someone could get Kyo started."

"Certainly sounds like a plan, but let's rest for a moment; I hunger!"

Smiling, Sira obliged, getting out a few meals she had packed for lunches. Once the other three had come back, soaking wet and smiling, they had a meal of sandwiches and carrots. Sira filtered the fresh water and filled their canteens, which were welcome, since the water tasted amazing.

With everyone satisfied, even Mia, who had gone hunting, they packed up what they got out.

Olivia looked up at the cliff, "Looks sheer. Are we flying up?"

Dom nodded, "Yup. Would you like to help Kyo?"

She responded by thrusting a rough gust of wind at Kyo, who caught it, *Easy, there; you don't want me to break my back on a tree, do you?*

"Nah, I knew you would catch it." She took off with Mia, leaving the others behind.

Sira tilted her head to the side, "What was that all about?"

"They had a little run-in this morning," Therin responded.

"And how would you know about it?"

She blushed and her face tightened, "I may have been slightly involved."

Kyo cut in, *Not that it really matters. Let's get going.*

Simultaneously, Kyo, Therin, and Ryan took off. Dom looked at Sira and shrugged, following after them. Being the only one with a different mode of travel, Sira's ascent was slower, but when she reached the top, the others were ready to go immediately. They started in a direction towards a cleft in between two of the mountains. Now that they were almost level to the base of the range, it was more apparent that that was most likely the best place to cross.

The sun had begun to set; the shadows cast by the mountains sheltering them leaving them in deep shadows. Sira glanced up at the gray peaks high above, a far cry from the damp valley they were traversing. The farthest she could see, just beneath the clouds, there were blankets of snow wrapping the tops of the mountains. From this perspective, the climb looked a lot steeper than it had before, so she was thankful they had the valley to cross through.

Mia, the leopard, was beginning to take on a more golden sheen, her black color wearing away to what was underneath gradually. Sira had no idea why it was, she just knew it would make the creature that much less stealthy at night. If they ever found themselves in a gold mine or a bright room, yeah, she would blend right in, but otherwise, the leopard was beginning to stick out. Besides, Olivia fully endorsed the familial relationship between Mia and the rest of the group, even she could only communicate with Olivia.

With the sun shedding even less light on their intrepid group, the surroundings took a more menacing view. Sira was reminded of how much the proper lighting might affect a scene, making different parts stick out if it was shaded differently. Now, the regal statues that stood guard over them morphed into hideous gargoyles, warning them to retreat from the place they so wished to reach.

Did Sira see movement in one of the recesses? Surely, it was her imagination; hers was especially strong. Especially in the dark. Especially when she had seen things recently, such as especially scary demons that especially wanted to kill her. That tended to be especially terrifying.

Therin and Ryan's animal ears twitched and they froze in their tracks. Therin shivered and looked up at the rock walls, "There something up there."

Dom shook his head, "Probably just a rabbit."

Sira rolled her eyes, "No, 'cause whenever this happens in a novel, everyone writes it off and then they get caught in an ambush or something; we can't be too careful."

Sighing, Dom looked at the walls himself, "Yeah, fair point. Shall we send one of us or go all together?"

"Let's send one at a time," Olivia counseled, "it'll create more suspense for Sira's book."

She blinked, "Huh?"

Now Olivia rolled her eyes. Maybe it was a virus of some kind, "Come on, you keep talking about event after event like they're parts of a plot, not to mention you have a 'highly accomplished lexicon'..."

"I did not say that."

"And now you're saying, 'when this happens etc.'. Before you know it, you'll be recording our every word so you can publish it."

So who's gonna check the walls? Kyo interrupted.

Sira silently sent her thanks via telepathy and got no reply, but judging by Kyo's slight smile, he was happy to help.

Dom ultimately made the choice, "I'll go; I've been here the longest, so I should have the easiest time with it."

They all nodded their consent and watched as Dom ascended to the level of a ridge, one that hid many recesses from full view. Something caught his eye and he glided into one of the openings. After a couple of worrying minutes, Dom's head popped out over the edge of the ledge. Huh, it kind of worried Sira that her narration automatically rhymed.

He spoke in a cheery voice, "Hey, guys, come check out this cave! There's diamonds and stuff!"

When the smiling face disappeared, Kyo shook his head, *WAY too obvious.*

Sira responded, *The intonations were different...*

He never uses exclamation points, Olivia pointed out.

Ryan rubbed his chin, *And he'd never let me know about any diamonds. Plus, I heard some scuffling, so, if that doesn't scream suspicion, I don't know what does.*

Guess we better see what's up there though. Oh, and rescue Dom. That could be important, Kyo decided, *Anyone wanna lend me some wind?*

Trying her hand, Sira guided the wind toward him as an experiment and found it was a lot easier now than it had been a while ago. When he caught it, she felt somewhat weaker, but quickly felt better, so she figured it was just a result of him using her as a jumpstart.

They took off gently, away from the wall when they came eye level with the cave, they were greeted by "Dom", who smiled at them almost unnaturally, as if he were taking a picture with which he was rather uncomfortable. He motioned for them to follow him vigorously, then he waltzed comfortably into a pitch-black maw of rock, swallowed alive by the blackness.

Olivia looked over to her and mimicked his smile and cheeriness, "Yeah! Let's follow him into the abyss to look at diamonds!"

Therin joined in, "I'm glad you agree, Olivia! I love walking into traps! I mean, caves!"

Despite the fact that their friend had either been possessed or cloned or something and was being used to lure them into the most obvious trap in existence, Sira couldn't help but laugh. Nevertheless, as she glided toward the ominous darkness, she kept her guard up, aware that a slip-up could mean dire consequences.

Upon entering the cave, Sira found that she could still see. There were two reasons that she found; one was the torches that flickered up ahead - another obvious tip off - and the other was, looking back, that Kyo was once again glowing, albeit only somewhat.

Ahead in the torchlight, Dom's face and smile were illuminated in such a way as to cause nightmares in Sira forever. And that was considering the demons she had fought. He beckoned slowly to them, still using his insane, happy tone, "Come on, guys! The diamonds are just a bit further!"

Looking up, Sira saw that there were holes in the roof above where Dom was standing, probably holes for rudimentary cages to drop out of or something. Humoring their soon-to-be-would-be captor, Sira took several steps forward, and she could hear the others following her. When she saw a larger room ahead, Sira began to wonder what fake Dom's original form was. A goblin, perhaps? Or a sort of chameleon demon.

Surprisingly, nothing fell out of the holes in the ceiling. Still on edge, Sira followed fake Dom, whose posture was too straight, into a wide room filled to the brim with cages, all filled with animals, humans, and humanoids.

Fake Dom threw out his arms, "Look at all of these pretty diamonds, humans!"

Behind fake Dom, real Dom was locked in a cage with his arms and legs bound, his mouth gagged, *That's not me, he's tricking you guys.*

Sira tried not to roll her eyes, but eventually succumbed to the virus, *Yeah, we kinda got that.*

Fake Dom continued, "What do you think of the pretty diamonds, humans?!"

There weren't any diamonds. The closest things were the iridescent scales of a naiad. Nonetheless, Olivia played along, more cheerfully than Sira could've, "Oh, we LOVE the diamonds! Where'd you get them?!"

Fake Dom exhibited an eviler, slightly less scary smile, though he still retained his happy tone, "You fools! There are no diamonds! There are only cages! And we will put you in one!"

Ryan tilted his head to the side, "As in, all of us in the same cage? 'Cause that could get cramped."

Confused, fake Dom fumbled over his response, "Yes, I mean no, we wouldn't be that inconsiderate! I mean, why have you stopped using exclamation points?!"

Rolling her eyes - what was it with eye rolling? - Therin responded, "Yeah, we've kinda been onto you for a while, fake Dom."

The fake Dom sighed, "Guess the jig is up. Boys?" He snapped his fingers.

All around them, lizard-like demons shimmered into existence, their scales shifting from the color of their surroundings to a dim purple. Sira had totally called the chameleon thing. The fake Dom also shifted into a demon, slightly larger and dimmer than the rest, but when he spoke, his voice may have changed to a raspier, deeper tone, but he still sounded like he was selling ice cream to kids, "All right, let's round them up!"

The lizard demons pounced. Obviously, they had a few advantages, such as numbers, a small space, and the element of surprise, but Sira and the others had strength, a tight group, and skill. Because the lizards had neither strength nor skill.

Tirelessly, Sira fended off each lizard that attacked her. Why they hadn't tried to capture them while they were still camouflaged, she had no idea, because she was easily mowing through them.

Sira threw a blade of rock against one, slicing off its arm. From behind, one tackled her and she was thrown to the ground. It started to try and punch her, but its aim was horrible, and she was able to thrash and dodge to avoid its fisticuffs. She wriggled one of her arms free and punched it up the jaw. It leaped back in surprise, leaving Sira free to stand, but the damage was done. Almost immediately, she was buried beneath several of the demons. The one closest to her began pinning her arms and legs and she could feel them being wrapped up in something.

When the heavy, scaly, elongated bodies slithered off of her, she was bound tight as a hog. Moments later, she was tossed into a cage and, despite the leader's promises, Ryan soon joined her, making it so that standing up or sitting curled up were the only mildly comfortable positions. She glanced over to Dom's cage and saw that Olivia was there with him. Casting her eyes about the tumultuous cavern, for the lizard demons were frantically running about, Sira couldn't identify Therin or Kyo. The slippery devils had probably snuck off with some trick or another.

But for now, Sira had to sit there uncomfortably, listening to the lead lizard's loud apologies like being bound without her full party was a minor inconvenience on a talk show.

She hated talk shows.

Chapter 9
Therin

Despite the fact that they were in plain view, the lizards continued looking for them. The weirdness was accentuated by the fact that Kyo was holding her hand with his own. How strange he would use his strong hands to wrap hers delicately - ugh, now she sounded like one of those love poems. Blech. She repeated "I have no feelings" to herself under her breath until she believed it. What a wonderful and enriching exercise.

Kyo pulled her slowly to a wall, out of the way of the lizards. While watching them carefully, he used telepathy to talk to Therin, *Don't talk out loud; we're invisible, but not inaudible. And I'm surprised they haven't smelled us yet.*

Well, they are pretty stupid. Can we talk to the others?

He shook his head, *I don't know if the demons would be able to sense traces of telepathy for whatever reason, so it's probably safer just to keep them in suspense.*

Do you have a plan?

It's pretty simple, just walk around to the cages and disintegrate them all at once.

Therin smiled to herself, *Then it's an all-out brawl. I like it.*

Without another word, Kyo started to move. Not wanting to risk a break in physical content for fear of the magic losing its potency, Therin followed close behind, careful not to make any sound, which was made easy by her bare feet. It was agonizing, treading slowly around the edge of the room, not disturbing any of the lizards.

When they were about halfway there, one of the demons walked right up to them, not showing any signs of stopping. Therin froze holding her breath. She knew she had to move, but she couldn't; if she were caught, their plan would be spoiled, but she couldn't will her legs to take another few steps to refuge. Someone pulled her arm sharply, and she remembered Kyo. He pulled her into a sheltering embrace, arms cradling her, letting her face outward.

She watched the lizard attach itself to the wall and begin to climb, eventually disappearing through a hole in the ceiling. Safe for the moment, Therin took a second to breathe. She squeezed Kyo's hand, not wanting to leave or get up or anything.

Eventually, he unwrapped his arms from around her, only holding her hand now, and they continued to creep in the direction of the nearest cage. He was blushing a little bit.

They finally reached the cage. Up close, it looked really fragile, but, based on the occupant, a creature with the body and horns of a cow and the tail and head of a mouse, it was probably a lot stronger than it looked. Kyo made eye contact with her, *Do you think you can get rid of all of them at once? And the bindings, too?*

No, problem.

Resisting the urge to pop her knuckles, Therin reached out a hand and touched one bar of the wooden cage. She imagined giving a team specific instructions for destroying the cages and bindings without touching the prisoners and she initialized the program of sorts with her Essence.

The first cage started to burn away, and when it was gone, the cages adjacent to it began to disintegrate as well. It was a beautiful chain reaction.

Not needing the cover anymore, Kyo let go of Therin's hand and they jogged past the extremely surprised lizards until they reached where the others had been tied up.

Standing up, Sira brushed herself off, "Took ya long enough."

Shyly, Therin recalled their brief rest, "We had a little run-in."

"Uh-huh."

Once Dom's bindings crumbled to ashes, he leaped up, ready to fight, "I've been waiting for this."

Ryan and Olivia promptly joined them as well, Mia close behind, all eager to partake in some demon-bashing. Unfortunately, the lizards were standing shell-shocked, staring at the disappearing cages with fear. Therin experimentally took a step toward them. All of them focused on her, which caused her to freeze once more. Instead of attacking, all the lizards turned toward the walls, scuttling into their retreats in the ceiling.

With the cave clear except for the other prisoners, Therin was disappointed, "Well, that was anticlimactic."

Olivia shrugged, "Agreed, but at least we don't have to fight all of them."

Dom nodded, also looking fairly put off, "Yeah, let's get everyone out of here."

It took a while to herd all of the prisoners out of the cave, but eventually, they got everyone outside. With a little wind and the climbing skills of some of the more able refugees, they were able to get the entirety of the travelers into the valley. After a while, the whole troop, marching with no rhythm, reached the edge of the valley, staring down at the large city in front of them.

Dom flew and addressed the crowd, saying that the six of them would go ahead and tell the inhabitants about the refugees, who would be following about fifteen minutes behind. Those in the crowd nodded their consent and Therin, Ryan, etc. picked their way to the front of the people, joining Dom and walking down to the city.

This city, unlike Daydream, looked a lot more modern, with skyscrapers, paved roads, and metal structures that appeared to be houses. There were all sorts of transportation, from wheeled vehicles to small, flying machines. It looked like the city of the future.

Therin turned to Dom, who looked confused, "What is this place?"

"Well, it's not Enrem, that's for sure. My best guess, it's probably Premoni, which is derived from premonition, probably hinting at prophetic dreams. This place will probably be weird, what with the combination of technology and whatever else is down there."

Sira started running down the hill, "Well, let's get a move on, guys! We gotta beat the refugees there."

Therin took off after her, with the others in hot pursuit. They reached the bottom of the hill and pranced across the plain, coming up fast on the border of the city. There was no wall to the city, but there were posts every twenty feet or so and there was a hum of electricity in the air.

Two flying vehicles shimmered into existence, pointing spotlights at the party, who had stopped near the invisible barrier. A voice boomed out of a loudspeaker, "Identify."

Heeding the command, Dom stepped forward and introduced them, then continued on, "There is a small group of refugees close behind us; about a hundred in number. Will you do what you can to help them?"

In response, the hum in the air died, "We will. Proceed with caution, for you are now in Premoni."

Dom pumped a fist, "Called it."

One of the vehicles descended silently towards them, turning and opening the door on its side at the same time. When it settled, a woman, dressed in a black business suit, stood up and beckoned them over. They obliged and she spoke to them in a hushed voice, "What are you here for?"

"Information," Dom responded, "about how to beat the Reaper."

The woman tapped her chin, "I may know someone. Get in."

Excited for the ride, Therin jumped up into the transport, which was sleek and circular. Inside, it was the same, all the seats smooth and round, but at least they had harnesses. She turned to the woman, curious about said harnesses, "So, how fast does this thing go?"

"It can reach speeds of up to three hundred miles per hour, but in the city, we're only allowed to go thirty for safety reasons." She stated it like it was automatic, as if she deliberately broke the speed limit on multiple occasions, "I'm Siko, by the way, nice to meet you all."

The others, including Mia, had all entered the transport as well. Olivia, petting Mia, addressed Siko, "Nice to meet you, too. You don't mind me bringing a demon into the city, do you?"

The woman raised an eyebrow, "As long as it's tame, but I don't see how that's possible."

"I have a few special abilities."

Siko just looked more and more curious, "What's your species?"

"Human, same with these goons," Olivia gestured to her companions. Therin was only slightly offended.

"What-" Siko cut herself off, "Excuse me, what's a human?"

Therin, confused at her ignorance, started to explain, but Dom cut her off, "A normally unexceptional being. Nothing more."

"Al-all right."

Therin was even more confused; not only had Dom cut her off for no reason, but Siko had presented herself as a professional until now, since she had just stuttered. Therin wanted to know why, *Dom, why-*

Many people here don't know what humans are, but they feel like they should be afraid when they hear the name. If anyone else asks, we're dark elves, since they're the closest to humans, as far as my research goes.

She elbowed Kyo, who was right next to her, *Did you hear that?*

Yeah, he told everyone that last part.

How'd you know there was a first part?

Siko clapped her hands, "Well, if that's the introductions out of the way, we should be able go into the city now to find your informant. If you would all take a seat and put on your harnesses."

Dom, making himself comfortable, voiced a question that had been on Therin's mind as well, "Who is this informant you speak of?"

Putting her hands on the controls, Siko sighed, "You may not wish to meet him if I revealed his identity. Besides, it's supposed to remain classified, so I shouldn't even be taking you to him in the first place."

Therin sighed heavily. And rolled her eyes, since that kinda went without saying. Slouching as much as she could with the restrictive harness, she gazed out the window as they took off with no more than a whisper. That at least was cool. Other than that, the view past the tinted glass wasn't really anything spectacular, just a bunch of buildings. Some were cool, since they swirled up in elaborate patterns, but they just left Therin wondering why such a thing was a thing. People are weird sometimes.

Leaving the side window, she stared instead out the front window, which was directly in front of Siko and Dom, the latter of whom was drinking everything in. The directions Siko took were disorienting, so that anyone who didn't know the route beforehand would get lost, as Therin certainly did. When watching the roads soon became hopeless, Therin instead watched Siko use the controls of the vehicle. They appeared to be simple, with a small wheel to steer with, which would also change the altitude when pulled up or pushed down. Two levers on either side of the steering wheel apparently adjusted the force the corresponding side of the vehicle put into the thrusters, the desynchronization of such would most likely assist in turning. Therin was good at figuring things out.

Eventually, they hovered over a nature park, one that had trees, walkways, benches, and the like, but it was vacant. Siko pressed some buttons, spoke a few unintelligible codes, and a circular pit began opening up in the grass. As they slowly descended into it,

Siko looked nervous, though Therin couldn't imagine why, if she had clearance and had been here before, as she obviously had, judging from the natural manner she had spouted the codes.

The darkness beneath the ground swallowed them and the hole above them began to close. The instant the last pinpoint of light disappeared above, bright lights flashed on all around them, making Therin blink profusely. As her surroundings came into clearer view, she realized that they were in a chrome hanger of sorts, where all sorts of vehicles, all unique from each other, were powered off, either hooked up to some sort of fuel container, receiving maintenance, or, in the case of one of them, had spotlights shooting out of it with evidence of popped balloons and confetti strewn about.

When they landed smoothly, the door on the side of the transport opened and Siko ushered everyone out. On ground level, ready to welcome them, was a procession of eight armored officials, all wearing a mask that was completely black, with no holes for a mouth, a nose, or eyes. They also all looked exactly the same; tall and skinny, but with wide shoulders, kind of reminding Therin of a hand shovel. Siko lead them onward through the escorts, who enclosed them smoothly.

They walked through the hanger, staring up or sometimes down at the various types of transports, which ranged from minuscule flying enclosures for one, or massive behemoths that were no doubt meant for many people. Experimentally, Therin tried to leave the escort to go get a closer look at a particularly interesting vessel, but she was blocked almost immediately. all right, so she had to go wherever the escorts took her. That didn't make her feel like a prisoner at all.

At long last, they reached a set of double doors composed of solid metal. The lead escort pushed through, opening the doors to reveal a long hallway stretching to either side. Therin groaned aloud; of course there would be more walking after the already expansive hanger.

After what felt like hours, the group came to a door that was plain silver-colored metal. It was locked by a keypad, a fingerprint scan, and several other gizmos. The four escorts in the front all grouped around the door, providing inputs around it, causing a chorus of unbolting locks. After the locks gradually came undone, the escorts stepped aside and gestured for them to enter. Dom, at the head of the group, entered first, followed by Sira and so on. Inside, it was slightly darker than the hallway, so Therin's eyes had to adjust again. When they had, everyone, including the eight masked escorts, was inside and the door was closed. Therin squinted ahead in the poorly lit room. At the end of it, not too far away, was a desk, the occupant behind it draped in shadows.

He spoke, raising a hand slightly, "Dismissed."

The eight escorts in turn took off their masks, revealing that they all had the same face; a man's with smooth features, so that it looked somewhere in between a man and a woman. They strode forward one at a time and placed their masks on an existing stack, swirling into a cloud and into the mouth of the group's ominous host. When all the escorts had been "dismissed", the man stepped into the light, showing that he, in fact, had the same face.

"Welcome to my office. My name-"

Siko interrupted, "Sir, is it truly wise to tell them?"

"Yeah, Agent Five, I think so. My name is Animus."

Chapter 10
Ryan

Uh, total twist there; Ryan was totally not expecting it. And, of course, the one person who Dom wanted to meet the least was the one who happened to be able to help them. Speaking of Dom, Ryan glanced over to him. He had a hand over his face and was shaking his head, evidently not liking the situation.

Dom gave an exasperated sigh, "Of course it's you. Do you know of anyone who has information about the Reaper?"

Animus chuckled heartily, "Heck yeah, that's me!"

Ryan thought that his accent had a certain ring to it. Faintly middle Southern, perhaps?

"Y'know, if I didn't know any better, I'd say that was a passive aggressive attempt to avoid me," his face darkened and his voice lost all traces of the accent, "You wouldn't try to get rid of me, now would you?"

Just as Ryan was shocked at the change in attitude, Dom also seemed speechless, but he managed to choke a few words out, "Sir, w-we'd be glad to accept any help you have."

The all-powerful being brightened up again, "Well, isn't that precious. Maybe it was my accent that irritated you, so I guess I'll stop that."

Ryan sighed, "Thank you."

"Careful," Animus warned, "you wouldn't want to show exasperation, now would you?"

"Uh, no?"

He shrugged, "Fair enough." He waved his hand and seven chairs appeared in a semicircle in front of the desk. There was even a cushy bed for Mia, "Sit down; I have a story to tell you."

Taking their seats, they all politely turned their attention to Animus. Ryan found the differences between him and Anima to be very major; while Anima was flowy down to her core, perhaps not counting her slightly masculine face, almost everything about Animus was rugged. His curvy face was covered with a five o'clock shadow, his clothes were bulky leather, and the muscles that showed were bulging and veiny.

Animus spun on his chair once before settling in, "Well, you see, a long time ago, there were three beings that presided over Dream. Those were Anima, the Reaper, and myself. We all lived in balance and harmony for a while until blah, blah, blah, tragedy, treachery, and undercooked waffles."

Unfazed by the comment of a poor breakfast experience, Ryan desired to know more than the rushed details, "Can we maybe know more than the rushed details?" He winced to himself; he certainly had Therin's eloquence.

"Why, certainly, good sir, if there are others who wish to hear the full tale?" He glanced at each of them sequentially, and they all consented when it was their turn, "Very well, I guess I'll tell you.

"Long ago, there were three powerful beings, each with responsibilities in Dream, where they watched over the land and the people in it. Anima and Animus, that's me, were a perfect balance for each other. We still keep the other in check, though she ends up scolding me the most, unfortunately. I hate that woman. But I digress; a while back, a few decades, centuries, or eons, whatever, the Reaper became dissatisfied with the attention he was getting. Or rather, the lack of it. It was mainly focused on me. It really didn't like how, since it was charged with maintaining the balance of Essence, that he had basically no job, so h- uh, it started making his job important, moving Essence around from one being to the other and fixing it, pretending it didn't know the cause of the disruptions.

"Eventually, I caught it in the act, with a little help from Anima. Together, we cautioned the Reaper that if it continued in what it was doing, there would be dire consequences. Of course, since she did most of the talking, it didn't listen, so we were forced to try and weaken it, but I fear we only made things worse. Now, it roams around, sucking up all the Essence it can from an area before moving on. For some reason or another, demons from regions it visits all follow it around, aiding in the destruction and relishing in the pain they cause.

"So, yeah, now we're here. I used to live in Enrem until a few weeks ago, when the Reaper sucked it dry; not even I was able to stop it. Anima says it's because meddling down here too much weakens my power, but I can't help it if a higher plane gets stuffy every now and then."

Kyo, thinking, turned to Olivia. Ryan could tell there was an exchange going on, but, since it was private, he wasn't able to hear it. Once they were finished, Olivia turned to Animus and began to speak, but he cut her off, "No need, I heard every word; I will give you help, but only in exchange for help that you can give me."

Typical; give a deity an inch and they'll pull you from the roots.

"Watch it, Ryan; I can read your thoughts. You're right to be resentful, but there are some places even one such as me can't go."

And where would that be? Kyo somehow managed to put irritation into his telepathy. Impressive.

Animus, oblivious just this once... for some reason... answered patiently, "I need you six to recover an item for me. It was stolen by creatures called Kiyengs."

Ryan's ears twitched, meaning that Therin had tilted hers too close to his ear fur, "What are Kiyengs?" She asked.

"Lizard demons. They typically live in caves where they trap their prey. They have great camouflage skills, but they're terrible actors."

Ryan face palmed, "How awfully convenient. Is the item perhaps a shiny diamond?"

"You know it. Did you happen to run into them on your way here?"

Sira sighed, slouching heavily into her chair, "Yeah, let's not talk about that."

Clapping his hands excitedly, Animus smiled broadly, "Well, then, looks like I don't even have to brief you about where to go! The only thing I have to say is that the treasure will probably be hidden up in their tunnels. You could either sneak in, or, with a little help, you could waltz in with metaphorical guns blazing."

Therin nodded her approval, "I like option two." She scared Ryan sometimes.

"Siko, get on that. They'll need thermal eyepieces and protective gear if you can find their sizes."

The woman, silent until now, stood up hastily and bowed, "Yes sir, as soon as possible, sir."

When she left, Olivia asked, "Any specifics on what this diamond looks like?"

Animus tapped the side of his head, "Ummm... it's shiny?"

"Very helpful," Ryan muttered under his breath.

"Oh, I remember, it's a simple blue crystal with a grip in the center. It should be fairly long. It'll look flimsy, but it'll be very durable. You could even use it as a weapon if you really had to."

"Very helpful," Sira praised.

The door behind them opened slightly and Siko's head poked out of the crack, "Sir, I've acquired various gear as you requested. I've even managed to secure an Essence pistol, which, for the benefit of the children, is loaded with batteries to fire blasts of searing Essence out of its barrel."

Dom looked impressed, "That'll definitely be useful. Perhaps Kyo could use it?"

Sounds good to me.

"Yes!" Animus exclaimed, "Well, you guys better get suited up. And be back with my crystal! Siko will escort you to the cave."

The woman saluted, "Sir!"

Ryan exited, Therin close behind. Piled outside of the door were several different piles of gear, some armor, some small weapons, but all had a headband of sorts with one piece of green glass on the left side.

Therin quickly walked over to the one meant for her and picked up the eyepiece, "Sweet, this will look totally edgy with my wolf ears!"

Ryan picked up his gear. Other than his eyepiece, he had long gloves made of metal plates. He tried them on and the plates on the outside of his arm expanded slightly into blades. Sweet. He tapped what looked like a button on the back of his hand, and they resumed being normal gloves. Or gauntlets, as was probably more accurate. He also had a sort of scarf. Siko helped him tie it around his face.

Once it was tied on, Ryan took a few experimental deep breaths, which the scarf didn't impede. According to what Siko said, it would also help him breathe underwater and would channel his voice when he whispered so only people directly in front of him would hear him. Pretty cool. Much better than Therin's bulletproof hoodie.

Still, with the lack of action, Ryan was a little disappointed, and his sister took notice, "How come you look so glum?"

"Why do I have to narrate preparations?"

"Well, you could keep narrating if you wanted to." She pointed out.

He nodded, seeing what she meant, "Yeah, but I feel like it should be someone else's turn. Besides, I feel like my character isn't really all that fleshed out."

Therin rested her chin on her fist, which was covered by the hoodie sleeve, since it was a little long. The hoodie kept slipping off one shoulder, due to its size, but Therin didn't seem to mind, "Do you want to progress your character right now?"

"No, it would just feel forced. For now, I'm happy to remain the somewhat cheerful, yet oddly quiet guy." He turned to the rest of the group, "Hey, who else wants a turn narrating?"

Chapter 11
Dom

Luckily, Dom was closer to Ryan when he called for a narration change, so he had gotten a hold of it before Olivia. After meeting with Animus, who was just as irritating as Dom thought he would be, Siko had herded them into another vehicle and shipped them out of the city. They retraced their route, even flying over the refugees just outside the boundaries. Outside, the sky was growing dark, and a few evening stars were coming out.

Dom looked back into the passenger section of the vehicle, which was more akin to a stealth plane than the circular one they had ridden in first. Along the aisle, the others were sleeping, trying to get rested up before infiltrating the Kiyengs' cave. Dom himself had tried to sleep, but had ultimately given up and joined Siko once more in the pilot's cabin.

She expertly guided the plane through the narrow chasm, which was wide enough to admit the plane, but only just. The silent thrusters carried them on a quiet course until they reached a point about halfway through the valley that Dom recognized. An opening in the rock, much larger than the others, yawned widely, seeming all the more ominous with the growing night.

The plane stopped and hovered just outside. Siko, pushing a few buttons, remained in a reverent silence towards Dom. He didn't want to break it, so he went to get up the others. Starting with Kyo, he reached out to shake him, but Kyo pushed his hand away, opening his eyes, *I couldn't sleep.*

That's understandable.

He shook his head, his black hair swaying, *It's not the stress; I couldn't stop thinking about the story of those two and the Reaper. It just sounds so familiar.*

It sounds familiar to me, too. It didn't exactly help us, but I guess it is useful information, except the part about the waffles, Dom offered.

I guess. You'd better wake up the others.

Nodding, but a little offended that the jokes wasn't appreciated, Dom moved from person to person, gently shaking them awake and helping them out of their seats. When they were all up, Siko pressed a button, opening a door in the side of the plane, "Go now. I'll be here when you return, but I'll be in stealth mode, so you'll have to signal. Just wave or something in my direction."

Dom nodded and led them out the door, stepping directly onto the ridge that would lead them to the cave. He sniffed the air, which was crisp and fresh, giving no hint to the rotting cages inside the tunnels. "Let's go."

Forging ahead, Dom called Therin up and told her to summon a flame for light. She did so and it produced a lot of light, but not much heat. How wonderful. When they entered the cave, the plan was to climb up the first tunnel they came across. If they were spotted, they would kill everything, but until that actually happened, they would do their best to remain under the radar.

Reaching the dark opening, Dom hesitated; would the crystal that Animus wanted truly be useful to them? Or was it just a ploy for the deity to gain more power? From what Dom had read about him, that seemed likely, but you could never tell. Perhaps he was trying to help them after all.

"Dom?" He looked back and saw Sira staring at him, worried, "Having second thoughts, are we?"

He shook his head, "No, let's get this over with."

Turning back to the gaping maw, Dom strode forward and into the domain of their enemies. Looking up, the cave looked a lot different than when he had been dragged through it, considering that Therin's flame lit it up to an extent. The ceiling looked a lot rougher than the walls, as if there had been less attention paid to it. Upon closer inspection, it was because there were carvings, worn away with age, but artistic in a sense.

The paintings depicted travelers all going the same direction, following a course along the ceiling. He looked ahead and above them, spotting the first hole. The paintings around there were larger, but they had the same proportions. It became clear to Dom that the travelers were becoming more lizard-like. Perhaps it wasn't a tale of a journey, but one of an evolution.

Dom stood directly under the hole, which was wide enough to admit two of them at once. He tapped a button on his eyepiece, activating a semi-transparent display of heat signatures, of which the vertical tunnel contained none. It came to his attention that they had no idea how to get Mia up there. He turned to Olivia, who was forming some sort of circle around the leopard demon. He looked at the girl curiously and she responded, a little irritated, "A gravity circle, so that whatever surface she treads on will be her gravity anchor. I'm thinking of making it permanent."

Dom nodded his approval, choosing to ignore her tone, "That'll be useful in the future, perhaps."

Kyo drew his Essence pistol and primed it. He touched Olivia's circle, too, probably to borrow some of the gravity change, *I'm ready, let's do this.*

With Mia following on the wall stealthily, Dom employed his new climbing gear, which consisted of gloves and shoes that contained barbed spikes that would cut through just about any rock, so he used them to crawl his way along the wall and then the ceiling, as if it were just the floor. Above him, in the tunnel, Kyo was scuttling along the wall at a faster rate, with Sira hovering close behind him. After Dom and Mira entered, Ryan also came walking along the wall, anchoring himself by encasing his lower legs in rock and wading through it. Olivia and Therin were the last ones to enter, ascending with a little wind.

Above them, Kyo and Sira were outlined by a faint light, which seemed enough to illuminate the tunnel. Dom transmitted, *Therin, snuff the light.*

When she did so, his visibility faded only slightly, so that only the area directly around him was obscured by the shadows. Continuing his climbing as silently as possible, he caught up to Kyo and Sira at the edge of the alien light, the others not too far behind him. Straining to listen, he caught the echoes of a soft conversation with a lot of hissing.

"Sssome kidsss were ssspotted outssside. Ssshould we ssstop them?"

Another voice, sssomewhat more human, even though it sounded practiced, unnatural, replied, "They should be of no trouble," Dom had decided to omit the extra S's, "though we should check on them just in case. I'd ask Chad."

"But Chad is always yelling."

"At least he can make decisions. Unlike some of us."

Dom dared not even whisper until the light faded somewhat and the sound of slinking footsteps slid out of earshot. He began to climb again, and the others followed suit. They reached the lip of the hole and peeked over, seeing a wide cavern, well-lit and full of building material, such as blocks of stone and scaffolding and planks of wood. With no living beings in sight, with the absence of both light and heat affirming this, the place was ominously deserted, which worked out well for them.

Rolling over the side, Dom got up in a crouch, retracting his climbing spikes. He signaled to the others to follow him, and, with stealth even Mia would be proud of, he began sneaking to one of the more shadowy spots in the cave, under the scaffolding against a rough wall. When he was across, he looked back and saw Sira, Kyo, and Ryan on their way, hastily tiptoeing over the open area. They all made it safely into the safe spot. Olivia, Therin, and Mia were next, all crawling, Therin's ears alert for threats.

Dom winced every time torchlight reflected off of Mia's gradually changing spines, casting dim ripples of light on the floor and walls, no doubt making it easier to spot them. At least her new saddle was considerably more low-key.

Therin's ears turned toward a specific spot and she froze, breaking into a run, she gestured hurriedly at Olivia to pick up the pace. Dom could only think of one reason why. Therin, since she was barefoot, was able to run almost silently, but Olivia's boots made a faint clicking sound when they hit the rock beneath. In addition, her new poncho, though black, was quite reflective with its weaponized material. On the walls, the lizard-like shadow of a Kiyeng overtook a large portion of the carved stone, "Hey, who'sss there?"

Olivia, Therin, and Mia all crowded into the shadowy shelter that the structure provided. Holding their breath, they watched as a Kiyeng slithered on its two wavy legs into their line of sight. It was holding a torch, so all it had to do was-

"Wait, you're not supposed to be here." It was looking right at them, reaching towards its belt.

Dom acted fast, jabbing his fingers like he was immobilizing a pressure point, forcing a thin point of wind into the scales of the Kiyeng like a bullet, punching through scale and skin. He unclasped his jagged sword from his side and hurled it at the stunned demon, puncturing its heart and instantly and silently dissolving it. He willed the sword back into his hand as if it were a strong magnet.

A troop of Kiyengs came from the other direction and pointed at where the sword had entered the shadow. One of them ran back, whistling, while the other three stayed behind, staring at the group in hiding.

Sira sighed, "So much for a stealthy mission."

Kyo shook his head, *Oh well, guess we'll just have to kill them all.*

Therin smiled, "I wanted option two, anyway."

Same here.

Dom chuckled, "Don't be so nonchalant about it; people might think you're a psycho."

So what if I am?

"Then we're going to need it." Dom stood at his full height and walked out of the cover of darkness, making the demons, who were several yards away, flinch back. When the others revealed themselves from behind Dom, they almost fled in terror, but a flood of reinforcements from the tunnel behind them and from where the first one must have come boosted their morale.

Looking back and forth between the horde and the group, Therin rolled her eyes, "Well, now this fight is almost even."

A certain Kiyeng stepped forward, "Pitiful humans! We would welcome you to our home, but you appear to have killed one of our own! Maybe we should kill them in return?!" Chad addressed his subjects, who all cheered in approval. "Very well, let's get ready to rumble!"

Dom groaned, "I really hate that guy."

The first Kiyeng to charge was a smaller one, with others behind him. Dom leapt forward and planted his sword between the eyes of his opponent, and those on the other side stepped around the quickly crumbling body to have their own shot at Dom, but he wouldn't have it; he twisted, pulling his sword free and slicing through his other two assailants in one smooth motion.

Dom looked up to find that he was completely cut off from the others, since the whole swarm had scuttled in between where he was and where the others were apparently spreading out. He summoned a little wind to gain altitude, rising far enough above the Kiyengs that they couldn't reach him. Around him, it was more evident that everyone else had voluntarily split up, each taking on a crowd of Kiyengs single handedly.

Therin climbed scaffolding with one hand and both feet while she used her other hand to fend off pursuers with a recently acquired telescopic spear. She stabbed downward at those climbing after her and she stepped onto a platform, gaining more stable footing for battle.

Ryan was nowhere to be seen, but occasionally, a bulge in the rock floor moved under a Kiyeng, sprouted spikes, and receded into the ground. Ryan was probably okay.

Dom saw Sira, who was plowing through demon after demon, flipping and cartwheeling, serrations appearing on her gear in the most opportune places, giving her acrobatics an edge, so to speak. She was surrounded by a halo of water, which occasionally hardened into a razor disc of ice. Sira manipulated it expertly, using both her arms, since it was about as wide as one of her arms was long. The disc, along with her gear, paid no heed to the demons' scales.

Olivia, riding Mia expertly, was hanging on to the leopard with her legs as it ran up the wall of the cavern, pursued by more than a few Kiyengs. With her hands, she was holding a pouch filled with the scariest dust Dom had ever heard of; it was nearly invisible when she threw it down at the chameleons, but when it seemed to make contact with them, it immediately turned blood-red and began to dissolve through them. Holes bored themselves into the Kiyengs and spread, causing the entire creature to slowly liquefy. If one of their kin were unfortunate to touch even the smallest drop of dissolved lizard, it caused a chain reaction. Soon enough, the demons chasing Olivia had to take long detours to get to her as the remains of their comrades sizzled and dissipated against the unaffected rock.

Amidst a swirl of glowing energy, Kyo stood still. Kiyengs, obviously the densest ones, threw themselves at him continuously, getting instantly vaporized by the ring of power. Other lizards, the smarter ones, threw projectiles at him. These, depending on their composition, were also disintegrated. Other, harder projectiles, like rocks or boomerangs, were deflected at intense speeds, killing the assailant. Kyo's Essence pistol appeared to have a link to the energy, which seemed to be instantly charging it, so Kyo, when there was a lapse in deflectable projectiles, would conjure his own with deadly accuracy.

Speaking of projectiles, a sharp rock crashed into Dom's left arm, snapping him out of his stupor. Oh, and also snapping his arm. The stinging pain raged through him, stabbing at his concentration. Through the haze in his eyes, he could see his arm dripping blood on the Kiyengs below, the majority of them producing bows, arrows, and slings from the pouches on their backs. Dom glanced behind him, and sure enough, there was another swarm of Kiyengs climbing up the wall to get above him.

His arm throbbed and Dom's wind shell flickered. He sighed at himself; he'd had enough of the drama. He sheathed his sword quickly and waved his now free hand over the wound. The pain heightened for a moment, signifying the cellular regeneration being galvanized. However, Dom felt his concentration slipping even more. He had a sense of falling. He tried to fly, he honestly did, but Dom was unable to form a wind current to keep him aloft. He braced himself to get speared on the Kiyengs sharp weapons… but it never happened.

Confused, he realized that what he was now lying on wasn't rock. In fact, Dom felt like he was floating. It was cold and wet. Moving his hand around, he realized that Sira had caught him in a floating pool of sorts. Gathering his wits, he sat up and looked around for her. There she was, hacking through the Kiyengs towards him, using three long knives, sometimes orbiting, sometimes in her hands, beautiful and deadly all the time.

On the wall, Olivia was running alongside Mia, apparently finding it easier to fight whilst not caring for the laws of gravity. She was leaping around, spinning within the crowds of lizard demons that had been aiming to pounce, lacerating them head to toe with her crow-like poncho.

Dom felt a tap on his shoulder and he jumped. Looking behind him, he saw it was only Sira. She dropped his puddle and formed her water halo again, letting him fall hard on the rock. She seemed playfully irritated, "Would you mind helping out? These guys don't seem to be thinning out much."

"Fair point. I guess I'll save my friends from imminent death."

"That's what I like to hear," Sira looked at him a little longer before dashing back into the fray, leaving a trail of lizard dust behind her.

Dom brushed the dust off and drew his jagged sword once more. He charged the air with electricity; his hair stood on end, electricity arced between the points of his sword, and the smell of ozone dominated over the smell of melting Kiyeng. His sword hand now shaking, he charged at the nearest demon and drove the sword into it, causing lightning to erupt out of it, which formed several chains. These chains ruptured the ranks of lizards, vaporizing many. Dom continued like this, blasting enemies into oblivion. It felt… somehow familiar, as if he were used to having to destroy demons. Then again, he had been in a couple of fights before, so it was probably nothing.

Between strikes, Dom heard a lizard-ish scream and the swishing of dust. He whipped around and saw Ryan, who had emerged from underground and smitten a Kiyeng that had snuck up on Dom. That made three times he had been saved. He was really bad at this, despite it being familiar.

Ryan glanced over his shoulder, "Time to go?"

Dom searched the walls around him for an exit, using his peripheral vision to defend himself. There were definitely an endless number of demons pouring out of the caves and swarming the walls; there wasn't going to be a simple end to this mess, "Yup. Let's find that crystal."

"Ten bucks says that leader guy has it."

Dom smiled. Only Ryan could make bets in the midst of fighting for his life, "I'll have to take you up on that."

Don't have to; I got it.

He surged upwards on a swiftly formed wind to see a fiercely glowing Kyo pushing through the swarm. Well, pushing was a little inaccurate. It was more like he was wading through the swiftly forming piles of ash and dust at a brisk pace.

Surprised at both Kyo's distance and the overwhelming din, Dom had to ask, "Can you hear everything we're saying?"

Yup. Must be the fact that it's echoey in here and you have a pretty distinct voice.

"Oh."

Somehow, Kyo mimicked a laugh in telepathy, *Don't be ashamed, just follow me. Not too closely, though.*

Dom looked over at Ryan, who was elevated on a rock spire, twisting his fox ears about to listen for threats as they waited for Kyo to pass them. Evidently, he had been given similar instructions. He scanned for the girls. Olivia was practically pulling Mia along at an inconceivable pace at the other end of the cavern, Therin was swinging from loose ropes on the scaffolding, and Sira was torpedoing in her water halo in their direction. She was probably going to be particularly dizzy.

Kyo finally got close to them and it was now obvious why he didn't want them following closely; the fierce glow was some kind of energy or heat, which was what was killing the demons as he ran through them. Dom swooped down at what he thought was a comfortable distance and swept through the few Kiyengs that were dumb enough to pursue Kyo, simply hoping the others would follow.

A Kiyeng leaped at Dom from the side, but it was almost instantaneously impaled with a long, black spear. It retracted and Dom followed it to Therin, who was effortlessly in stride with him, "C'mon, slowpoke; anyone could've seen him coming from a mile away."

"Thanks," was really all he could muster.

Therin replied, "You're welcome," before increasing her pace to get closer to Kyo, whose glow was fading. Dom just wondered how that girl could run so fast. Sure Olivia was faster, but that was her whole thing.

Kyo was apparently leading them to a dark cave with few surrounding Kiyengs. There were many ropes from the scaffolding snaking into the cave, but beyond that, Dom couldn't see very far into it. Ahead, Therin thrust her hand upward, casting bolts of flame to either side, taking advantage of the rather convenient ropes. The resulting blaze provided just enough light by which to see the uneven cave floor, but it cast long shadows over the group, creating the illusion that they weren't really there. It was unnerving, and it made Dom wish for a faster way out of the cave.

The flames from the ropes petered out and Therin burst into flame. It wasn't hot, so it must've been purely for the purpose of illumination. They continued to run, not missing a beat. For a while, the Kiyengs relentlessly followed them, popping out of holes in the walls or catching up from a direct pursuit. Always, they were cut down, melted, impaled, or disintegrated.

Ryan groaned in frustration. Dom was behind him, but he was sure Ryan was rolling his eyes, "I'm sick of these things."

Ryan slapped the rock wall behind and all around them, Dom heard the echoing sounds of stone scraping against stone, indubitably closing off all routes to them from the main cave. He stumbled and Dom caught him, picking him up and carrying him on his back like a fireman would.

"Sorry, Dom. I overdid it again."

Dom shook his head, "Don't worry about it, just rest. You've earned it."

He felt a sharp hit on his head. He looked up to see Olivia hanging upside down, riding Mia on the ceiling, retracting her hand. Evidently, she had flicked him to get his attention, "Hand him here; Mia can take it."

Ryan, though weak, still resorted to banter, "Are you calling me fat?"

"Maybe."

Dom hoisted him up as best as he could without breaking his stride, which he found to be quite difficult, "Wouldn't it be much easier to perform this exchange if we were both on the natural ground?"

Olivia seized Ryan and strapped him into the luggage part of the saddle behind her.

"Oh, so I'm baggage now, am I?"

Olivia sighed and her head tilted suspiciously. For her, there was no hiding an eye roll, "Stop flirting and start fainting from overexertion."

Ryan obliged, probably from a combination of actual exertion and just being fed up with talking to Olivia. If he was being honest, Dom could relate; the endless running through the winding tunnels was rather taxing on his muscles, but at least there weren't any slopes. Nothing was worse than a full cardio workout complete with slopes to kill your legs.

Ahead, the tunnel was being lit by a more natural light, the faint silver of the moon. Dom was instantly re-energized with the hope of escaping the winding tunnels. All together, almost in stride, they rounded the corner to be greeted by fresh air and a high view of the other side of the valley, the mountain opposite them towering far above them. The half-moon was just barely breaching the peak, allowing it to shed its light within the valley. Kyo fired a shot from his pistol out of the mouth of the tunnel and the bolt exploded like a firework. Probably what worked as a signal for Siko.

It occurred to Dom that something was wrong with this picture; hadn't they entered the mountainside at a much lower altitude? He looked closer at the exit to the outside. Sure enough, it dropped away even before the walls and ceiling came to an end. How amusing.

Ahead of him, the others had doubtless noticed the same drop off, for they were jumping off without hesitation. Kyo even performed a swan dive off the cliff. Dom himself merely jumped off. The wind rushed by him until he commanded it into a vortex around him. As his descent slowed dramatically, he scanned for where they had originally entered the cave so that he would be able to signal the plane, which was evidently still in stealth mode.

It turned out that he had no need to look, for the sleek black plane suddenly materialized below them and began to rise to meet them. Dom flew down, following the others. Most everyone was flying, but Mia had to leap from the rock wall onto one of the wings, her gravity shifting seamlessly. Under the silver moonlight, her spines, which were now almost completely golden, seemed to glisten, reflecting the light which had already been reflected from the sun. Dom reflected on this reflection briefly, but decided it was a more prudent use of his concentration to approach the open hatch in the side of the plane.

When he was inside, he saw Kyo showing Siko the crystal. It was clear and had a simple leather handle wrapped around it. One side was long and slender, shaped like an obelisk. The other side was short and its curved edges appeared to be sharpened well. Animus wasn't kidding when he said that it could be used as a short-ranged weapon.

"May I look at it more closely?" Siko asked.

Kyo nodded and handed it over. Only then did Dom notice that there was a faint blue glow about it. As soon as it changed hands, the glow faded. Siko raised an eyebrow at this, but said nothing. She looked it over for a couple seconds, but soon handed it back to Kyo, "You should hold onto this until we can pass it on to Animus."

Kyo stuck the crystal into his belt and used sign language to reply, translating to the group as he did so, *But you technically led the mission.*

"Me? No, it was all about you six the entire time," Siko protested, "Besides, I need both hands to fly us back to Premoni ASAP."

Dom's heart skipped a beat, "Why, what happened?"

Siko walked into the cockpit without replying. Almost as soon as she did so, the plane tilted precariously and began to maneuver much more vehemently than on their flight to the valley. Immediately, everyone leaped into the closest seat and buckled up. No sooner had they done so when the plane did an acrobatic spin, throwing Dom against his seatbelt and roughly back into his seat. He looked out the window and saw a wave of falling lizardmen, who had evidently climbed onto the plane.

Once their vehicle leveled out, Dom practically tore his seatbelt open and he forced his way into the cockpit. "What exactly is going on?"

Siko had no need to answer verbally. She merely pointed out the windshield ahead of them. Dom followed her finger and had his worst fears confirmed. The reaper, larger than ever, had come around the north of the mountains and was now on a course to swallow Premoni.

And if they didn't get out in time with the help they needed, it would swallow them as well.

Chapter 12
Olivia

Okay, so now they were on a death trip towards a city that would soon be eaten by an overwhelming entity that would leave their bodies as a pile of lifeless ash. If Olivia was keeping track of the days correctly, it was Saturday. She loved weekends. And of course, there was nothing like the threat of death to finish off a week of dodging demons and conquering caves.

Now she merely had to wait for the plane to land in the bunker, but since they had only just reached the city limits, it was going to take a while, knowing Siko. Why Animus hadn't rendezvoused with them outside the city, Olivia had no idea. It was going to be extremely inconvenient to walk out of Premoni with a demon hoard and a dome of death in pursuit.

As Siko made her evasive way through the city to protect the base's location (what was the point of that, really?), Olivia impatiently stroked Mia's spines. She had noticed a while ago that doing so rubbed more of the inky blackness off of her now golden spines. What little black did rub off this time faded within a couple seconds. If a cat was going to shed its overcoat, Olivia would've wanted it to fade away. She was glad she didn't have to worry about her clothes being stained black. Then again, looking at her attire, black on black wouldn't have really mattered.

She heard her boot heel clicking beneath her. She hadn't realized she was fidgeting, but now it was obvious. Was she really so anxious? Olivia forced her heel to stop moving, but the fidget almost immediate shifted to her fingers, which drummed on her cheekbone as she leaned on the armrest. She sighed; it was going to be a long flight.

Ryan sat down next to her. In the past few minutes, he had recovered his senses and awoken tied to Mia on the ceiling. The site of him struggling with the latch on the luggage strap had been amusing, but eventually, Olivia had had Mia come down and she helped him out of it.

Olivia looked over at him, "What is it?"

He smiled, "Oh, nothing. Just thanks for lugging my useless body around while I was unconscious."

"Is that all?"

Ryan laughed. A peppy laugh that was kind of out of place considering the situation, "I suppose you do look more glum than usual."

Olivia rolled her eyes, "Don't worry, I'm only miffed we're having to get even closer to that orb of death since last time."

"Oh, so it doesn't have anything to do with Therin and Kyo chatting over there?"

She practically jumped out of her seat, "What?!"

It was true; across the aisle at the front of the plane, Therin and Kyo were staring at each other, most likely having a telepathic conversation. Every now and then, Therin would snicker and Kyo would smile, as if they were sharing jokes. The nerve. As if Therin had the right to be happy while they were flying to a near-death situation.

She felt a hand on her shoulder. Olivia turned her head and found that it belonged to Ryan, who was calmly smiling, "Best not to interrupt. If I know my twin sister, she's having a good time."

"How did you get to be so grown-up?"

He shrugged, "I have a friend named Aly. Hanging around her kinda grows you up."

Olivia sat back down, deflated. She stroked Mia's spines again. The leopard sent feelings of comfort toward her and images of open fields. That's what communication with Mia was like, since she didn't have a language. She merely sent what feelings or images she decided would best fit. Or, at least, that's how Olivia figured it worked.

"You know," Ryan started, "if anyone looked hard enough, they might guess you're jealous."

"Jealous? Me?" Olivia rolled her eyes, "Anyone can have a good time."

"I'm not talking about Therin having fun."

"Oh." Then it hit her, "Oh. Oh no, am I that transparent?"

"Well, it took me this long to notice you liked Kyo, but I didn't really wanna talk about it until you noticed yourself."

"Just now?"

Ryan nodded, "Just now."

Olivia sighed. She thought back on it and realized that Ryan was right, she did have a crush on Kyo. And so whenever he and Therin talked, it just sort of set her off. But why should she? Even if they both came from the same world, they were years apart, so Olivia really shouldn't bother. How's that for depressing? When she wasn't thinking about getting eaten by the Reaper, she was brooding about her non-existent love life.

Trying to brush it off, she asked Ryan, "So, what about you? Got eyes for anyone here?"

He shook his head, "Nope. I'm not really into the romance stuff."

"Fair enough."

Olivia resumed looking out the window, though not for long. Apparently, Ryan had distracted her for long enough that she hadn't noticed that the plane was already in the bunker and was about to land.

Siko came out of the cockpit, "Everyone get ready. The meeting needs to happen fast."

Olivia stood up and bolted to the door, casually sliding up to it. The others, rather slowly in her opinion, followed suit. There wasn't the slightest bump to give any indication that the plane had landed, but the door opened right next to her, sliding to either side. At the bottom of a ramp stood Animus, waiting with two of his clone guards. Siko ushered them down the ramp.

In rebellion, Olivia hopped onto Mia and asked her to walk down on the underside of it. She obliged and Olivia clung to her the whole way down, her hair eventually brushing the floor of the hangar before Mia switched gravities again. Animus seemed amused, contrary to the impending doom.

He opened his arms to greet the eight of them, counting Mia and Siko, "There you are, right on time. Was the mission a dead-on success?"

Everyone looked at Kyo. He walked forward slowly and presented the crystal to Animus, who glanced back and forth between Kyo's face and the crystal, which had regained its blue glow. "Interesting," he noted, "Very interesting."

His gaze fixed on Kyo's eyes. The concentration and the tension in the air between them was enough to hint at a silent conversation. It was infuriating how often these were happening. Animus' eyes never left Kyo's but his hand reached down and plucked the crystal out of the boy's hands. But before, as with Siko, the glow didn't fade. In fact, it intensified.

"Siko," Olivia almost started at how much more powerful Animus' voice sounded, "detain them and jettison them from the city."

"Yes, sir."

Dom exploded, "What?! After we went through all of that trouble, you're just going to throw us away? I thought you would help!"

Animus chuckled, "Oh, but I am helping. I'm going to use this crystal to take back what Anima took from me so I can get rid of the Reaper. And as far as I know, Kyo here acts as a repellent to the Reaper, so you're gonna be safe no matter what happens."

We don't know how long I can repel it or, if I do it for long enough, if it'll find a way around it.

"Well, I guess you're gonna have to find out. Siko, immediately."

"Yes, sir, sorry, sir. I just wanted you to finish the conversation, sir."

Animus rolled his eyes, "I figured. Only every evil henchman uses that as an excuse."

Siko's eyes grew wide, "Sir?"

More of the Animus clones materialized around Siko and the others. One grabbed Olivia's arms and shoved them behind her back. They were surprisingly strong. When she reflexively struggled, an electric shock coursed through her, briefly knocking her out. When she woke up again, her vision was black at the edges, but she could still work out that she was shuffling along a corridor, being pushed by one of the clones. She didn't dare look behind her for fear that would trigger another shock, but she could see ahead that Ryan and Siko were also being roughly escorted.

They rounded a corner and came to a row of small hatches. Siko was shoved into one on her own. It closed behind her, her escort pushed a button, and there was a loud beep that sounded. The artificial light from beyond the window in the hatch gave way to natural light. Olivia was pushed past it, but she could see that the window had a direct view of the Reaper.

Ryan was shoved into the hatch directly after the jettisoned pod, and for a moment, Olivia feared that they would all be launched separately to their deaths, but that fear was quelled as soon as she was pushed into the same pod. She sidled into the seat next to Ryan as Dom, Kyo, Sira, and Therin were subsequently manhandled into the pod. Therin was half asleep. Apparently, she had been a lot of trouble. Mia was practically thrown in, her unconscious body limp, but alive. With all of them in there at once, it was pretty cramped. What made it worse was that Animus, along with four of his clones, filled the space beyond the hatch.

Animus himself spoke a bit too cheerfully, "Don't worry, we'll launch you in a direction far away from the Reaper. Siko merely gave me cause to dispose of her. Finally. She was getting pretty annoying; 'Sir this, sir that', on and on and on."

Olivia blinked, "But how will you get away from the Reaper? You've wasted all of this time trying to get rid of us."

Dom was the one to answer, "Apparently, Premoni is a flying city. We took off while you were out."

Animus nodded, "Yup. And I've got this to use." He held up the crystal, which had continued to glow fiercely. "Well, I'm done with my monologue. Well, I wouldn't really classify it as a monologue. More of a summary of what's gone on up until now. Anyway, tata!"

As he reached for the eject button with his other hand, however, Kyo reached out as if he was reaching for a lifeline. The crystal flew into his grasp just as the hatch shut and the pod launched from the port. It began to glow even stronger, almost blindingly. Kyo tapped the long end of it with his finger and the glow dissipated. *There we go, that was getting annoying.*

Dom sat up, getting used to the speed of the pod, "Okay, what now?"

Now we escape; this pod is going to be ripped to shreds by the demons even before the Reaper gets to us.

Olivia held up her hands, "Wait a minute, I'm behind. Why did the crystal obey you?"

Therin drowsily agreed, "Yeah, what's up with that?"

Kyo looked at the crystal, the thing for which they had fought so hard. *I don't know. I just had a distinct impression that it was mine, but I know that sounds egotistical.*

"Whatever that means," Ryan rolled his eyes.

Anyway, everyone ready?

"To do what?" Olivia asked.

To fall to our deaths.

Sira smiled, "Heck yeah."

Everyone looked at her.

"What? I needed a line. You guys get to talk for forever."

Dom sighed, "Fair enough. Do you want to do the honors?"

"Umm... oh, you mean to bust us out. Yeah, sure, I guess I can do it." Sira maneuvered her way to the hatch and placed her hand on the edge. She began moving her hand around it, creating a sheet of ice over the whole thing. Once it was completely encased, she busted it in with some of her razor-edged armor.

Wind burst through the new opening and it was as if Olivia's friends were all sucked out one by one, but they had all voluntarily jumped out. Mia, who was conveniently aroused by the loud rushing of the wind, twisted up and sent of image of her and Olivia going out, making use of the gravity circle. She obliged and practically leaped into the saddle in the same instant that Mia leaped out the hole in the wall, her trajectory curving to match the outer shape of the pod.

The leopard landed on the outer armor of the vehicle. Around the pod, everyone else was using various methods of slowing their descent. Olivia didn't feel comfortable leaving Mia to fend for herself, so as the pod plummeted to the earth, Olivia stayed with her companion. The ground came closer and closer and she kept putting an image in Mia's head of the cat jumping from the pod at a precise moment.

The ground still came closer and then Mia jumped and twisted in midair, her gravity shifting to *terra firma*. That gravity circle was really handy.

Olivia looked for everyone else. Ryan and Dom were together near some isolated trees while Therin, Sira, and Kyo were making their way over to the other two boys. She followed them astride Mia, who galloped across the tall-grassed plain with ease.

The trees marked the beginning of a foothill, the foothill, the beginning of a mountain. Animus had launched them south. Not exactly out of the line of fire, but close enough. Speaking of Animus...

Olivia glanced back at Premoni and gasped. She hadn't expected much of what was going on. For one, the entire city was flying high above the ground. High above the Reaper, even. The aforementioned gray dome of death was stagnant beneath the city ship, like a fox patiently waiting for a bird to land on the ground. Clouds of little black things, most likely demons -- though it was hard to tell from so far away -- swarmed around the large engines in the bottom of the city. One by one, the engines failed and Premoni was slowly eaten up by the Reaper.

It happened right before Olivia's eyes. Something that she knew was going to happen, regardless of how. The city was almost entirely gone now. A light flashed brightly, like a star going out, and the Reaper grew significantly in size. At a guess, Animus, the brute, had just been served for dessert.

With the city gone, Animus gone, and any help for their quest gone, Olivia sagged, the weight of it all pressing down on her. She couldn't help it. Tears started to come to her eyes. She blinked and wiped them away before anyone could see. She turned on Mia so that she could join the others, but found Ryan standing there, tears in his eyes. Eyes that were fixed on the menacing enemy. Eyes that swiveled to her.

She was conscious of her eyes still being moist, of his being the same. But she didn't care. If he had shown his weak side to her, shown that he, too was scared of the Reaper, then she had no choice but to encourage him. She hopped off Mia's back, strode up to him, and slapped him in the face.

"Ouch!"

"There, now we're even."

Ryan looked as confused as he was mad, "For what?"

Olivia rolled her eyes, amused, "You're not depressed anymore, are you?"

He narrowed his, "No, I'm just mad and in pain."

"Well, there you go. Now, stop brooding and let's join the others. Again."

"I came over here to ask you to do that."

She laughed, "Well, I'm doing your job for you. Let's go."

Olivia climbed back onto Mia and they joined the circle that was being formed. Nothing like a meeting with an all-powerful vacuum and its pet creatures from heck on the horizon.

Sira spoke first, "I say we retreat and regroup."

Dom nodded, "Agreed."

Agreed.

Everyone else gave their affirmation. Apparently, it would be a very short meeting with an all-powerful vacuum and its pet creatures from heck on the horizon.

Everyone else turned and ran; Sira leaped into the air using platforms of ice, Therin literally blazed a trail through the grass, Ryan surfed on dirt, Dom flew low to the ground, and Kyo merely ran. Almost as fast as Olivia could on her own. "My, they grow up so fast, don't they Mia?"

The leopard sniffed in impatience beneath her.

"Fair enough, let's go."

Mia leaped forward with an exuberance that was yet unknown to Olivia, as if the darkness that had rubbed off over time had left Mia much lighter so that she could run like the wind. They quickly overtook Kyo and passed him.

Could you turn off your leopard? She's blinding me.

Olivia laughed both from amusement and exhilaration. *Is she really glowing? I hadn't noticed.*

You must already be blind.

Briefly, Kyo flashed into Olivia's view just ahead of her, then disappeared from sight completely. That boy was cool. Maybe that's why Olivia liked him so much. Or maybe his hair, his personality, or the billion other cliché things to say. Heck, Olivia annoyed herself just thinking about all the reasons why he was cool. She shook it off. Best not to think about it.

Ahead, Olivia spotted something. A dark shape in the grass. Mia scraped to a halt, having seen it as well. Olivia remembered her eyepiece, which she flipped forward and turned on. There wasn't just one dark shape, there were many. A blockade, in fact.

She notified the others via telepathy, and they all converged on her spot defensively. They all turned on their eyepieces and surveyed the thermal signatures. Some were familiar, like Kiyengs and other demons they had already fought, but most were unknown or hard to discern from the way they were waiting in ambush.

Olivia scanned in front and around them. The demon army seemed to go on for miles. On impulse, she looked up and found a host almost as numerous as the first. She turned back north, the direction from which they had come. The Reaper was bearing down on them, even closer now than it had been before they had begun moving. How was that even possible? Had consuming Animus given it that much power?

Whatever the case, Olivia now knew that their situation was next to hopeless; an inconceivably large demon army on the ground, an armada in the air, and in pursuit, the Reaper, which was faster than them at their full speed.

They were hopelessly outnumbered, outmatched, and surrounded.

Chapter 13
Aly

Aly sighed and turned off her tablet. She had exhausted all of the games on it and now all it did was bore her. The only thing that was ever a different experience was the group chat, though no one was on, so naturally, she was reluctant to pretend taking care of a simulated farm was fun. She checked the time, which was 6:52, Friday night. Grandma would leave soon to get her own dinner.

She rubbed her neck. It was still sore, but it was feeling a lot better. She straightened her gown and wrapped her blanket around her. Aly didn't want to get out of the bed to just walk around the room for a few feet. That was boring. Besides, they made her get up and walk this morning, so what was the point of stretching her legs if she would just have to get out of bed anyway in the morning? She hugged her stuffed animals, old things that hadn't left her side, even in the transition from home to here. Supposedly, they would also go with her to the mental hospital once a bed opened.

Aly shuddered at the thought. First of all, she'd have to sleep in someone else's bed for who knows how long. Again. Second, those places kind of scared her. A mental hospital? As if she were some kind of insane person. Maybe they would send her home and forget about her. Who knew? Not Aly, that's for sure. She worried one way or the other, since she'd never had a pleasant experience with doctors.

She heard a knock at the door. Another doctor or nurse? She didn't know if she could handle any more of them. However, the door didn't open almost immediately, so it couldn't have been personnel. In fact, Grandma had to get up and open the door. When it opened, Aly forgot about everything on her little bed and leaped out of it. She practically tackled her visitor with a hug. He chuckled and hugged her back.

"Easy, Aly; I'm not as young as I once was."

"You keep saying you're old, Zach, but you're not even an adult yet."

Zach rolled his eyes, "Yeah, and you're not even twelve yet." He turned to Grandma, "I'm not too late, am I?"

She shook her head and smiled, "No, not really. I was going to head out, but I can call a member of staff if you want to stay longer."

He nodded, "If you could when you leave, that would be nice."

Aly pulled him over to her bed and sat down. He sat down on her left. She noticed the bag he was carrying and pointed to it, "What's in there?" Zach almost always brought presents when he visited. And they were always exactly what she wanted or needed. A new stuffed animal, food, books, all of them useful.

"What, this? Nothing important," he claimed.

"I don't believe you."

He laughed, "Okay, you caught me. These were really hard to hunt down, but I managed to find some." He reached into the bag and pulled out a package of some weird kind of pastry. He noticed something on her face, "Canelés, made without rum, of course, so they're gonna be more savory."

"Is that what they look like?"

"Yup."

"And you're obsessed with them because of that anime you watched?"

He sighed, "Yup. I still can't believe one of my most otaku friends still hasn't watched it."

Aly pointed to her tablet, "It's kind of hard when your only source of entertainment is that hunk of metal."

Zach snickered.

"What?"

"Nothing. Just that you calling it a hunk of metal reminded me of another show and…" he smiled broadly. He always had that face when he was remembering a private joke with himself.

"Which show?"

"Even if I told you, you wouldn't get the reference."

"Maybe if you told me, I'd watch the show and then I'd get the reference," she reasoned.

He smiled again, "Have you ever watched a show I've recommended?"

Aly shook her head, "Nope."

"There's my point."

She smiled and lay back on the bed, spreading her arms out. She looked up at the same ceiling she had seen every day for the past week. Thinking about how long she'd been cooped up, it was a mistake. She should've done a better job.

Zach was staring at the wall when he asked, "What're you thinking?"

She got defensive, "Nothing."

He looked at her, worried. She tensed up under those eyes. The color shifted as often as their purpose. Sometimes they were blue, sometimes green, or sometimes grey. And sometimes they were comforting, sometimes they were distant, and sometimes, like now, they were searching. He didn't search long, "Your neck looks better. The purple spots have all disappeared."

Her hand reflexively went to her neck. She had had purple spots from the screaming, but no physical repercussions from anything else. It was the panic attack that showed outside, "Thanks, but that's obviously not why I'm in here."

Zach smiled again, this time in comfort, rather than in jest, "I know, that's why I'm here for you. I'm glad you told me about it."

She looked away, "It was my plan to not have to tell anyone about it ever again."

Aly flashed back a week, to the rope, her dad catching her, literally and figuratively. She had screamed her head off because she had wanted it to happen. She had set it up, because she had just been so hurt, she finally couldn't take it anymore. As she recalled the memory, the hurt came back and tears welled their way into her eyes.

"Aly."

She looked back at Zach. Just seeing him there, tall, but not scary, was comforting, but now his eyes, too, were moist. He barely seemed able to choke out the words he was whispering, "I'm here for you. As a brother."

Aly was taken aback; they were friends, but she had always felt closer to him than any of her other friends. Not in a romantic way, but it was something different. Now he had identified it and she was content with it. She sat up and gave him the biggest hug she could muster, her tears now flowing freely.

He hugged her back, softly, like he was shy. Of course he was. Even when he was being open with her, he always held back. That's how he always acted. Aly pulled out of the hug, "Thank you," she whispered back.

He smiled and turned back to Grandma, "I hope, that wasn't too awkward for you, Grandma."

The older woman took out her headphones and looked up from her book, "Huh?"

While Aly suppressed a laugh, Zach came up with a white lie, "Nothing, we were just wondering when you were going to go."

Grandma looked down at her watch and started, "Oh dear, if I don't leave now I won't get home until very late! I'll go get a member of the staff so you guys won't be alone."

He brushed it off casually, "Aw, don't worry, there's a security camera to keep us company." He pointed to the back corner of the room, where a small black dot was embedded into the wall. How had Aly not seen that? Oh, that was embarrassing.

"No sweet talking me. It may work with Aly's mother, but I see right through you." Her tone was playful, so Aly knew she didn't mean it.

Zach pulled the blanket around his left shoulder and flipped it up with his right. Aly got the message and pulled it around her right, then they leaned together a bit. He went on, "Then we'll just be here doing nothing until the nurse gets here." He smiled broadly and innocently, almost as if he were half his age. Sometimes, Aly wondered if he acted this way with every figure of authority.

"Fair enough," Grandma concluded before she strolled out of the room.

Aly looked Zach in the face again. He waited for Grandma's footsteps to disappear. As he did so, his fake smile faded. He was so good at acting. She tapped him on the shoulder, "What's this really all about?"

He turned to her, his face not really blank, but not really showing any emotion, either, "I brought you another present."

She tilted her head to the side, curious, "But it's secret, right?"

He nodded and reached into his pocket, "You know how Ryan fell into a coma a few weeks ago?"

How could she forget? It was one of the major events that had... pushed her over the edge. She nodded.

Zach pulled out a small white card, under the blanket so that the security camera couldn't see it, "It took a couple tries, but I was finally able to swipe one and make a copy so that... well, so that you'd have a bit more freedom at night."

Aly smiled and almost cried again, "Which room?"

"308. You'd have to sneak out late at night, and between increments of fifteen minutes starting at two minutes past midnight."

Her head practically blew up just then, "How did you figure that out?"

"The last time I visited around lunchtime, I saw that there's an employee that kind of does a patrol of the floor, morning and night, every fifteen minutes. They always start at around twelve sharp. At the rate they walk, they'd pass your room in two minutes at the very most."

Aly laughed, "I guess stalking is a talent of yours."

He smiled back, "You might say that."

She hugged him again, "Thanks, it really means a lot."

Zach patted her on the head affectionately, "I know, that's why I did it. Just don't get caught, or they'll know it was me."

"How come?"

"Because I'm the only one other than your family who visits you. And I hang around the halls for a bit before leaving or after coming in. And because the world is biased against teenagers."

"You're almost eighteen," she teased.

"Don't remind me," he rolled his eyes. He always got mad whenever anyone brought up his age. Well, "mad" might be exaggerating a bit. "Mildly annoyed" might be more accurate. But she always wondered why he was like that. Maybe it had something to do with how they were such close friends, but thinking like that made Aly's head hurt.

"I just hope seeing Ryan like that doesn't set anything off for you."

She looked down, "For the last time, I'm doing better."

He laughed good-naturedly, "You say that like it's a bad thing."

"Maybe it is."

Shaking his head, Zach objected, "No, getting better's only allowed to be bad for me."

She hit him lightly, "Oh, stop."

"What? It's the only way to get you to cheer up."

They continued to banter for a little bit about who was more depressed until a nurse came in. Luckily, she was one of Aly's favorites, the one who always put an extra pudding with her lunch. Aly's conversations with Zach continued to be open, but not quite as open as they were before, as now they had an audience that was watching everything Zach said and how Aly reacted to it. All in the name of a speedy recovery.

She and Zach could talk about pretty much anything, from anime to old shows to art. Books to food to personal goings-on. Right now, they were talking about their creative works. Zach had brought a copy of his novella that he had just written for her to read. Aly showed him the notes she had written down for her fanime. He glanced over them with what looked like careful analysis, with the occasional smile thrown in. After he saw them, he merely said it was a good idea.

"That's it? No 'it's weird' or 'it's missing a few details'?"

He blushed and turned shy again, "Well, you should know by now how bad I am at giving critique."

She groaned, but accepted that he wouldn't go further than that. They continued chatting for a good while longer and ended up sharing the canelés. Aly had never had them before, but she loved the sweet, crisp outside and the savory, doughy inside. Zach might have just gotten her addicted. Before long, half the case was gone before Aly decided she'd had enough. Zach politely backed off and stopped eating them, even though she could see him eyeing them from time to time.

Barely any time had seemed to pass before Mommy came in. And not much longer after that, visiting hours were over and Zach was told to leave. He respectfully did so, even bowing in courtesy. Aly rolled her eyes; he kept claiming he hadn't watched a lot of anime, but from the way he acted, it was almost as if he was a blend of all the characters of the ones Aly had watched. Maybe it was just a coincidence. It probably was. He barely knew any Japanese, anyway.

After he left, Mommy settled into the recliner with a book and a blanket. She tried to make some conversation with Aly, but it wasn't the same comfortable environment with Zach. She had noticed that everyone treated her like she was fragile and carried her with a net, cushion, and wadded blanket around her. Zach, however, treated her like she was fragile, but held her directly, without stifling her in padding. Wow, that was a really deep thought for her. She'd have to share that with him. He'd put it into a book somehow.

Mom eventually stopped trying to talk and merely told Aly to go to sleep. Mommy laid back and turned off the light and used a reading light. Aly turned away from her and toward the door. Under her blanket, ever so sneakily, she set her alarm for 3:02 AM on her tablet, giving her mom plenty of time to fall asleep before it would go off. She pulled out the headphones that Zach had smuggled in and plugged them into the jack. She stuck one in her right ear and laid the right side of her head on her pillow, making sure everything was hidden. Then she fell asleep.

She woke up six hours later to a peppy anime opening song blasting in her right ear. Aly quickly turned it off and turned over slowly to see if Mommy was asleep. The reading light was apparently left on, as she could see it glowing dimly about where Mommy's lap was. From the reflected light, Aly could see her mother was breathing with a steady rhythm. That's all she needed.

She rolled out of bed, her bare feet coming into contact with the cold tile. They made very slight sounds as they pulled off the tile each time she took a step, but even she could barely hear it over the sound of the air vents. Walking to the door, Aly pulled the key card from out of her gown pocket. She opened the door an inch, just enough to peer out to see if the employee or nurse or whatever had passed by yet. When she couldn't see them, she opened the door a little further and looked the other way. Aly could make out a silhouette wielding a flashlight heading down the hall. She was in the clear.

The reading light was needed, since it was a small, dim light source that wouldn't immediately give her away, so Aly snuck back to get it. It was a battery-powered clip on light, so all she had to do was pull it off of Mommy's book and she would be able to use it. After she had it, she snuck back out.

Using the reading light and after a little trial and hour, she figured out that room 308 was… seven doors down from her in the opposite direction the patrol person was going. Had he really been that close the whole time? And how could she say she liked Ryan if she had never visited in the first place. But he was in a coma. That might make her uncomfortable or worse, even more depressed than she already was. Maybe it wasn't a good idea to sneak out, after all.

No, she had to do it now or never. Who knows when she'd be transferred? She pushed the door open and let it fall back closed, listening for the soft click as it did so. She forged down the hall, holding the light against her chest. When she came to one of the dimly lit doors, she pointed the reading light at it to check the number. 312... 310...

308.

Aly took a deep breath and swiped the key card in the door. The pad beeped quietly and the red light turned green. It worked. She turned the handle and quickly stepped into the room before she got caught. Inside, it was quiet, somehow quieter than her room.

Quiet, except, for a steady beep.

Aly looked at Ryan's bed and saw that he was hooked up to a pulse monitor, which, if she was guessing correctly, was showing good data. A brainwave scanner showed what looked to Aly like a lot of activity. That was weird. If he was in a coma, why would his brain be so active. At least she knew he wasn't dead.

Glancing around the room, she saw a recliner identical to the one in Aly's room, only this one was occupied by Ryan's dad. If Aly were to guess, and if her information was correct, then Therin was asleep across the hall with most likely her mom in the room with her. Why Zach hadn't mentioned that, she'd never know.

Content that the only adult in the room was asleep, Aly moved closer to Ryan. He looked so peaceful. She longed to be able to be at peace like that for once in her life. When she thought about when she'd first heard that Ryan had been in a crash, well, her life had just gone downhill from there. First, she couldn't talk to Ryan and at first didn't know why. Then she found out through Ave that the twins had fallen into a coma. Then Zach stopped talking on the group chat. Then school started to pile up. It seemed like a domino effect, not even stopping there. Eventually, she had decided that choking to death would be better than continue living in that sort of heck, but that had made it worse.

But Ryan was still so... serene. Aly, as if it would comfort her, reached out to touch his arm. Then she blacked out.

Chapter 14
Ryan

She appeared right next to him. One moment, Aly wasn't there, then poof, she was standing right next to Ryan. She looked as if she was lost, though he supposed popping into a mystical world of dreams after falling asleep would do that to you. It was a bad time, though. He was glad to see her familiar face, but not outlined by the Reaper's dome.

She blinked once, twice, then burst, "Wait, what?!"

Everyone else turned towards her, wondering where the new voice had come from. When Therin saw her, she ran up to Aly and gave her a hug, "Aly! What are you doing here?"

"Umm... I don't know. One moment, I was visiting Ryan and then I was here. Did I... fall asleep? Is this a dream?"

Ryan smiled. He had been exactly the same way when he and Therin had woken up here after the crash, "We'll explain later. We just have to get away from that." He pointed at the Reaper.

Aly looked at it and her eyes went wide, "Yeah, let's go."

Olivia stepped off of Mia and asked hurriedly, "But how? There's the Reaper there, demons in the grass ahead of us, and demons in the air blocking our escape. There's no good way out."

"Could we take a messy way?" Dom asked.

Therin pumped a fist, "Yes."

No, Kyo interrupted, *We don't want to endanger whoever this is. Aly, was it?*

Everyone looked at her. "What? Why're you all looking at me?"

Shoot, I forgot I wasn't linked to her. Olivia, would you please?

She nodded and stepped up to Aly, "Now this might hurt a little bit, but we've got to do it sooner or later."

"Huh?" Aly recoiled at Olivia's touch to the side of her head, "Ouch! What did you do to me?"

Connected your thoughts to me.

"Woah, he sounds like..."

Ryan pointed at him, "That's Kyo. Since he's mute, he has to communicate through telepathy."

Okay, now that she's at least a little caught up, the only clear path is over the Reaper.

"What?" Sira interjected, "I'm not comfortable going close to that thing. Though, we are pretty close to it already."

She was right, for as long as they were talking, the Reaper had closed the distance between them enough to make Ryan even more worried. That thing was fast.

That settles it, let's go.

Aly held out her hands, "Wait, hold on, I am most certainly not caught up. I don't know what the Reaper is, why we have to run, how we're going to go over it. Can someone explain stuff to me?"

Kyo walked up to her and went down on one knee so that they were about level, *Listen, for now, you just have to trust us. We'll get you out of here, and then we'll talk.*

Aly hesitated, but she nodded, satisfied at least for now. Kyo looked at Olivia, *We could use a diversion. Could you and Mia--*

"On it." Olivia hopped on her mount without hesitation and took off, the two of them a gold and black blur in the distance within moments.

Ryan stepped forward an launched himself into the air with a rock spire. From there, he manipulated the wind to thrust him upwards. He heard Aly exclaim below, but it was quickly carried away by the rush of the air around him. Next to him, Dom was using a new method of mobility, causing lightning to arc between him and the few clouds, which he then rode, like he was being pulled up by a rope. Sira was using a water halo which swirled around her, lifting her like a helicopter. Therin, being Therin, just flew.

Kyo, below them, seemed to be having more trouble. He was lifting not only himself with wind, but he was pulling Aly behind him, who was trembling with being up so high. Ryan stopped and started to descend to see if he could help, but Kyo glanced up at him with a look that meant he didn't want any help.

Convinced, Ryan bolted back up, as fast as he could, moving towards the Reaper as he ascended. As he neared it, he began to ache all over, as if his muscles were being pulled toward it. Frightened, he focused on ascending more than advancing and soon felt the pull fade. He wondered if, had he strayed too close, would it pull him in until he couldn't come back? Like a black hole?

He shuddered at the thought and flew far above where the crest of the dome was. Ryan wouldn't be taking any chances. The others leveled out around him, Kyo coming up last with Aly in tow. She was making progress, not screaming and kicking around. She looked as if Kyo might have taught her the basics to manipulating her Essence, since she began to float around a bit without any extra effort from Kyo.

Ryan looked at Kyo, waiting to see what else he might say about their escape plan. He'd noticed that, but for a while now, Kyo seemed the one to be drawing up the plans, taking over for Dom. He just seemed so... powerful.

He caught Ryan looking, *What?*

"Just wondering what to do next."

An arrow from behind Kyo just missed Aly. Coming through a wisp of cloud, a few flying demons wielding bows appeared, growling menacingly. Kyo looked at Aly for a little bit, who then nodded and let go, shakily floating in midair. He pulled out the crystal and the Essence pistol. He handed the latter to her and brandished his own weapon towards the demon squadron. It began to glow and rays of light burst out of the end. Each one homed in on a demon, changing direction with its target. Once each of them was vaporized, Kyo turned about, grabbed Aly's free hand and pulled her at a blazing speed past Ryan.

He took that as a sign to follow. Ryan tried his best to be as fast as Kyo, but, naturally, it was impossible. However, he was able to get a good view of what was going on below. A streak of gold was cutting swaths through the demon foot soldiers, if they were organized enough to call them foot soldiers. Every now and then, they would retreat, drawing off the demons and calling attention from the demons above.

Ryan looked around as he continued following Kyo, watching for any demons that might attack him or the others. A few stragglers from the initial armada that they had spotted were following them, chasing them with arrows that were able to catch up when the assailants themselves couldn't. But Ryan wouldn't be impaled by a common arrow today.

Instead he twisted and faced the pursuers. He threw out his hands and a wall of air formed from clashing currents. He left himself open and the demons launched their arrows all at once. He felt the tips, made of stone, his easiest element to manipulate. Each arrow turned in midair and ripped through its owner, effectively dispatching of them.

He turned back to fly forward faster and nearly crashed into Kyo, who had stopped and was looking down. Ryan quickly saw why. The Reaper was getting closer, but it wasn't because it was moving along the ground towards them, it was moving up.

The Reaper was flying. The darker steering node within it was visible, pointed directly at them, somehow pushing the Reaper off the ground. It was no longer a dome, but now was forming a sphere, perfectly round. The sight of it frightened Ryan more than the pull at the heart the entity forced upon him, for now, nowhere was safe from the Reaper. Wherever they went, it would follow, unabated by any terrain, grounded or in the air. Demons, they could handle, but this? It was too much.

Until Kyo became a *deus ex machina*.

The older boy held out the crystal with both hands and closed his eyes, concentrating hard. From the crystal, a small orb began to form, but it steadily grew larger, enveloping him, then Aly, then everyone else. It wasn't an orb, but a shield. Or at least, Ryan hoped it was a shield.

The Reaper was close now, too close for comfort. He braced himself to flee in case the shield didn't hold. But he didn't have to worry about that for very long, for when the two spheres collided, the Reaper made a hissing noise and began screeching violently. It was the same noise that it had made that night so long ago when Kyo had first stood against it. He forced it back now with the shield and everyone was now safe inside it.

Everyone, that is, except Olivia.

And the demons knew it.

What few had still been chasing Ryan and company now gave up on their efforts, turning back to the ground. Beyond the crackling shield, he could see that there were more demons than he had ever seen converging on one point. A point where there were golden flashes and black streaks.

Ryan tried to warn her telepathically, *Olivia, you need to get out of there now!*

Awww, can't I ravage a few more legions?

No, there's to many of them heading towards you. Just look around!

The black streaks paused and Ryan could imagine seeing her glancing back and forth between the sky and the ground around her, the thrill of battle giving way to the dangerous panic of being cut off, *You're right, I'm surrounded. I need help.*

Ryan turned to Dom, "I'm going to help Olivia!"

He looked down at the cloud of demons, then at the sphere around them, then around the Reaper. He gave Ryan a thumbs up that said, "Okay, but be careful."

He shot off toward the land, the shield letting him out like a microscopic organism, the wall morphing its shape around him and closing back up immediately after the toes of his shoes pulled through. His human ears were too full of rushing wind to be of much use as he reached terminal velocity, but his fox ears were still sharp enough to pick out Olivia's cries and yells, more desperate than confident now.

As he got closer, Ryan met with flying demons. He came upon them, their backs still turned. He tore through them with the serrations on his armor, not even slowing his descent by a moment. Ryan's collision with the earth was inevitable now; even if he began to slow, it wouldn't be in time. This was how he planned it.

He crashed into the dirt, which condensed under him, changing its shape to cushion his landing. The excess land was morphed into sharp spires, which erupted all around his newly formed crater. Everywhere he could feel a demon, he commanded a spire to skewer it. Around him formed a crater, a minefield, and a graveyard all in one.

Before the dust even cleared, Ryan unsheathed his curved sword. He bolted forward, planning to get Olivia out as soon as he infiltrated the demon ranks. They knew they were being attacked now, as some were entering the dust cloud in order to avenge their fallen comrades.

Big mistake.

He could feel them as they entered, and he commanded the earth in the air to collapse around his enemies. Ryan leaped over the rock-clad bodies without a second thought. Already, he was ripping through minotaurs, veget-eagles, dark leopards, and myriads of other demons to rescue his friend. All around him, the ground exploded, fragments of rock pelting assailants like shrapnel, disabling or even killing them.

Slice that demon, impale another, always pushing forward. Ryan kept pushing through. He noticed the crowds getting thicker and Olivia's battle cries getting louder. *Olivia!*

About time. I think I've got--

Her thoughts cut off, but Ryan doubted it was because she had more pressing matters on which to focus. With increasing prejudice, he massacred his enemies, but now he could see into the circle they had formed. Within it, several demons, urchin-leopards all of them, were crouched over something, trying to tear into it. As he watched, Mia came racing from somewhere unseen, radiance to confront shade. The cat-like demons turned from their prey to the dissenter, the golden one that stood before them. Ryan could almost feel the hatred in the air even as he raced towards Olivia, forcing back other demons with earthen walls.

Before Ryan could destroy them for trying to maul her, though, they all leaped at once at Mia. The demons that had seemed so intent on Olivia now converged on the golden leopard. Ryan was left almost alone with nothing but Olivia's broken body to keep him company. He stumbled over to her, pushing through the stampede, not killing for fear of being trodden on himself.

He picked her up, which was not easy; she was so laden from dust and dark blood that had rubbed off on her from her battles that it was hard to lift her in his arms. She coughed weakly as he took off from the ground, "Sorry, I guess I should have gotten out sooner."

Ryan smiled back, "You're alive, that's all that matters."

She smiled too, but remembered who had been with her, "Where's Mia?"

He gulped, knowing that Mia was gone. There was no saving the leopard, even if he went back for her now. Instead, he continued to ascend towards Kyo's radiant haven. Olivia's eyes widened, knowing what this meant, that her friend had fallen. She closed her eyes, letting a few tears escape, but she said no more. Ryan looked back as he got further up, being able to just glimpse the dispersal of the demon hoards. From their center point came a faint golden glow. All that was left of Mia was now as dust in the wind.

He felt the sphere of light embrace them moments later, Olivia still cradled in his arms. Dom and Sira came towards him, holding out their hands to take Olivia into their own embrace. That made sense. Dom was better at things than Ryan and Sira, having power over water, would -- for some reason dictated by the universal laws of elemental powers -- be better at healing.

Only now did Ryan see that Kyo was moving the sphere, which made sense. He could see the demons gathering at the edge of the protection and the Reaper pressing against the barrier. The sphere itself resisted the Reaper, pushing it back and forcing it to produce that awful wailing. It seemed as if they were well protected, but that couldn't be true.

Even if Kyo's barrier could never be exhausted, they merely had to wait for his physical body to tire and for him to fall asleep. Then his concentration would be unable to hold up the barrier and... Ryan didn't want to be surrounded when that happened.

Everyone, hold on to me.

Still shocked at what had happened, was happening, and might happen, Ryan merely obeyed, not even caring what the end result would be. In the end, he took hold of Aly's arm. He could feel her tense a bit, but he still didn't care.

Even when the world turned into a blur beneath them, he still didn't care.

Chapter 15
Dom

"So that's it, huh?"

Dom nodded. He had just finished explaining to Aly how everything worked; Essence, the Reaper, pretty much everything. Everyone else was resting around a makeshift campsite in the middle of the day, which was perfectly understandable. Kyo had collapsed, Olivia had cried herself to sleep, etc. Pretty much, Dom had been free to catch Aly up with all that she'd missed without interruption. It had been pretty easy, since Aly listened well and seemed to comprehend it easily.

"So, if I wanted to, I could summon a scythe and transform my clothes?" Aly asked excitedly.

He laughed, "Is that an anime reference?"

She looked down sheepishly, "Kind of…"

"Theoretically, yes, you would be able to do that, but it would be pretty difficult. It would take considerable concentration in order to turn thin air into a scythe, not to mention transforming the matter of your clothing. Actually, I think your clothes are fine the way they are."

Aly examined them herself, looking over the fingerless gloves, the tight-fitting black shirt, and the equally tight leggings. All in all, she looked like she was ready to run in a triathlon or something. By the looks of her, she was only eleven, but the outfit made her look a couple years older.

Something came to him. A memory of a conversation he had with someone else a while ago, "You know, you remind me a lot of how Ryan was when I had to teach him about this stuff."

Looking up at him, Aly seemed confused, "Really?"

"Yeah, I mean, we all have a point where we need to learn from someone, right?"

"Oh, I guess you're right." She paused for a while, but again asked Dom a question, "Does Ryan ever talk about me?"

He thought about it a while. He hadn't had a lot of casual conversations with the twins outside of teaching them, since he had been so focused on learning about the Reaper. But in the few times he had talked to Ryan, perhaps Dom could remember something, "I recall him mentioning you a few times, but he never really went into much detail. I don't really know, though, since I kind of talked to him as little as I could."

Aly seemed disappointed, "I see."

Dom immediately felt like he had to cheer her up, "Don't worry, Olivia talks to him all the time. Once she feels better, you could ask her."

She pulled her knees up to her chin, "Yeah, Olivia talks to him all the time."

"What do you mean by that?"

Aly rolled her eyes, "Well, you just skipped right over his twin sister, and went straight to the friend he's made while he's here."

Dom tried to laugh to keep the mood light, "To be fair, Therin kind of scares me with all that fire."

She smiled at his attempt, but turned to the fire that was at the center of the camp. A thought struck her and she brought up a new subject. Dom had noticed that she was good at that, like her mind went in several directions at once, "So you can control Essence, which can control everything else, right?"

"Right."

"And each of you has an element that's easiest to control, right?"

"Right."

Aly smiled, like she'd come up with something revolutionary, "And what are those elements?"

Dom blinked. He certainly wasn't expecting that question, "Well, Therin likes fire, I'm comfortable with wind, Ryan uses earth, Sira uses..." He trailed off, suddenly realizing what was so funny.

"Water, right? Isn't that weird?"

Dom started to laugh, "Yeah. The only strange ones are Olivia and Kyo. She can run fast, unlocks telepathy, and can apparently change the direction of gravity. Kyo, however, can run even faster, disappear, and he glows a lot."

Aly blinked, "Yeah, that's a little hard to name."

"Maybe you'll finish off the trio of hard-to-name things?"

She huffed, "Hardly. I could barely keep myself in the air during that whole mess. I don't know how you guys do it."

Dom smiled, "It'll come with practice."

"Does what Za-- I mean Kyo did come with practice?"

He turned away so he could think about how to answer that question. Dom had been surprised with Kyo's every move today. The barrier, the speed, the barrage of light. At a guess, it all came from the crystal, but still, he had no idea how or why the crystal and Kyo could do that. Animus had talked about the crystal like it was really nothing special, but when he had it, it was almost as if he had felt like he was in control of everything. But from the beginning, Kyo was the one in control of the crystal. Was that because he was the first one to hold it after it was in the possession of the Kiyengs? Did it have some kind of succession principal? Perhaps. But maybe he should just ask Kyo when he woke up.

"Dom?"

Snapping out of his thoughts, he realized he'd been quiet for a long time, "Sorry, Aly. I don't know, really. We'll have to ask him."

She stretched out from her curled-up position, "Okay, but he's kinda scary."

"I bet he is, considering all you know of him is his battle prowess, but he's actually really nice."

"Mmm..." she stared up at the sky. The conversation was over, apparently.

That was all right with Dom. At the very least, it meant he could think about things. He was good at that. Like what they were supposed to do now. That was kind of an important detail. With Animus gone, they had no one that might help them. Not reliably, anyway. They could hope that Anima might give them some help, but that was a long shot, since she had such an excellent track record of being useless. There was also the point that all she seemed able to do was summon recruits.

Dom looked up at the bright sky, the large cumulus clouds billowing all over the aerial sea. At least the Reaper would be noticeable flying over them. Good thing it wasn't overcast.

A flicker of movement caught Dom's eye. A small white object with hints of black was in the sky. Interested, he stood up and shielded his eyes from the sun's glare. It looked vaguely familiar and it occurred to Dom to check it with his eyepiece. He did so. Sure enough, it gave off a heat signature. Though, now that he knew what the UFO was, he supposed the pronoun should be "she".

"Oh please, not her."

Aly stood up and looked where he was looking, "Who?"

"Of course I had to think about Anima. I practically summoned her with that train of thought," Dom shook his head, disappointed in himself. Sure, she was probably here to help, but after what happened with Animus, all-powerful deities just didn't sit well with him.

Aly remained expressionless, "So Anima's coming, huh?"

He nodded in response.

"How much you wanna bet she'll die, too?"

"Best not to foreshadow too much, Aly," Dom sighed.

"Fair enough. Should we get the others up?"

He looked around at everyone sleeping, contemplating what might happen if they did. "I'm not sure whom they would hate more if we woke them, us or Anima."

"Well, Kyo's never met her, right?"

"True, so he might be okay."

She clapped her hands, "Okay, I'll work on it."

Dom watched as she proceeded to rouse everyone from their slumber. When Kyo didn't wake up immediately, she resorted to shaking him and yelling in his ear. Ryan was awoken by yells, as well. By the time Sira had been deafened, Olivia and Therin were already shrugging off their own sleep. They were lucky they hadn't been assaulted by Aly's energy.

"So why did someone set the alarm clock?" Therin yawned, rubbing her eye.

Dom pointed as he responded, "A certain deity is making a house call."

Sira groaned loudly, "Ugh, not Anima. First, we had to deal with her counterpart trying to double-cross us, now we have to deal with her causing a rude awakening."

"Actually, it was Aly who caused the rude awakening," Ryan rubbed his ear to get his point across to everyone else, but he was smiling. Apparently, he was just teasing.

Aly giggled, "Most fun I've had all day."

Watching Anima approach, getting larger and easier to see, Dom pointed out, "It might be the only fun you have all day, if this goes the way I'm expecting."

Kyo's head tilted to the side, And how do you expect it to go?

"Horribly?" Olivia guessed.

"Horribly," Dom confirmed, "She may give us an impossible assignment, but she may tell us how exactly to complete our quest. Though, even if she does do that, I doubt it'll be easy."

Silently, they stared at Anima as she descended on their little camp, her long white robes actually touching the grass this time. Her bare feet seemed to hover just above, though, but it was nice she was making an effort to get on their level. Her cosmic hair was just as imposing as ever, making sure you stuck with looking at her face, so that you didn't get lost within the immense black and maze of stars.

She spoke and Dom felt as if his stomach were on the ocean, being pulled back and forth by the smooth waves of her voice. Sickening. "I've come to welcome the sixth recruit."

He blinked once, confused. Therin was the first to respond, "You're a little late for that; we've had six for a while now."

Anima seemed irritated when she replied, "Oh, have you now?" She turned to Aly, "I suppose your training is already complete, then."

Dom caught on, "Wait, Aly is the sixth recruit of yours?"

She turned to him, her dark eyes seemingly on fire, "Yes, and it took me a rather long time to get her into this world. Eventually, I was forced to put her into a comatose state, not knowing when I would next be able to locate you. When you had all left Daydream while I was still looking for your last companion, it distracted me in many ways. First, I had to find you in Dream, then I had to bring this new ally into this world. When I felt Animus' death, it was not hard to find your presences nearby."

Dom could see that these events had angered her a lot. If looks could kill -- though hers most certainly could -- she would have slaughtered them all where they stood.

"Wait," Ryan interjected, "if Aly's the last one, then what about Kyo?"

Anima's fire turned to the mute, "If by that name, you refer to that thing with which you have been traveling, then all I have to say is that he was never a recruit. I had expected you to complete your task without the aid of such creatures."

Therin stood to confront her, "What do you mean, Kyo's a creature?! You say that like he's not human. He's helped us out more than you seem to care!"

"I mean by that, my dear Therin, that he isn't human. And because of that, I would never have chosen him to oppose the Reaper."

Dom watched as Kyo walked closer to Anima, fingering the crystal strapped to his side, *For one reason or another, having this with me had restored some of my memories. It gives me a few ideas why you don't want me here.*

Dom was taken aback, "Wh-what do you mean, Kyo?"

Anima here? She started it all. It was her mistake that cause the Reaper to appear.

Sira gasped, "So you snatched us up in order to fix what you did?"

"I cannot do it by myself. I am bound by higher laws that you could not possibly know," Anima retorted.

Olivia huffed, "Yeah, I'm guessing you put those in place so you could be lazy. Either that or put Animus away down here."

A few of the stars within Anima's hair went supernova. Apparently, she was very angry, "If I had made such laws for such a purpose, I, too, would not be standing here before you."

Ryan pointed at her feet, "And yet you're not standing here."

Dom could barely hear Aly whisper, "Buuurn."

He figured it was time to shift the subject before Anima's hair caught fire from all of the stellar activity, "So if Anima accidentally created the Reaper, what does that have to do with Kyo?"

The boy in question turned to Dom, his black eyes piercing into his own, *Don't you see? I am the Reaper.*

Chapter 16
Kyo

He woke up to find a primordial world. He rose out of the chaos, the dark muck that would eventually form into something. What it was, Kyo didn't know, but at least he saw he wasn't alone. On either side of him, two other beings emerged from the darkness, one was a woman, the other a man. They were both wearing white robes. Kyo turned his eyes downward and found he was clothed in the same. He didn't have to talk to them, he knew them, as if they were the same person, all three of them together. The woman Anima, the man Animus, and their bridge, Kyo.

Together they waited in the sea of black while an image began to surround them. It faded in slowly, over what seemed like many hours. Kyo could feel the light breaching the murk, the breeze as it was no longer held down by clouds of darkness. His bare feet touched the red grass, which was sharp and itchy. He didn't mind, though. It felt as if it were a rough, shaggy carpet, which was rather comfortable to him. Wait, what was a carpet? Whatever it was, Kyo felt like comparing the grass to it.

He watched further as more and more of the image materialized. Below, at the bottom of a hill, there was a city. How was there a city if the world was just created? Could the city be older than him? But that was impossible; by just a few minutes, he was the oldest one in this world, beyond the receding black nothingness that had surrounded him at first.

Kyo felt the urge to descend to the city, controlling a sort of fall, as if changing altitudes was as simple as thinking for him. He knew Anima and Animus were following him, his companions.

When they arrived at the walls, they could see that it was still being formed. It was not older than the three beings beholding it, it was merely being created as if it was. Perhaps that's the way the entire world, as Kyo could feel it, was being made, entire civilizations and landscapes that would've taken millennia simply appearing out of nowhere, but the way they came into existence was… right. Each area that would've seemed out of place was the way it should be.

Beyond the planet, Kyo could feel the formation of… what, empty space? What was there before, the overwhelming darkness, simply wasn't there anymore. Now the darkness he felt was natural, not oppressive. He concentrated and could feel further away from the newly formed planet. Reaching out, all he could feel were two massive objects; one, rather close, was the moon; the other, so far away, was the sun. He looked up with his solid eyes and what he saw didn't match. He saw the moon, full and bright, but he also saw so many stars. He couldn't feel them, even when he reached out as far as he could go. Then he hit a boundary through which he couldn't penetrate.

If this was all there was, how could their universe exist? For some reason, Kyo felt he knew that this small area of creation would fall apart relatively quickly without more to it. How he knew, or why that knowledge was there, he had no idea. But it was not the only bit of knowledge he had; already, in the short time since his creation, he knew much about how the world around him worked. He knew about people, minds, biological behaviors. There was so much knowledge that he had that he had been created with, that he knew that it must be for a purpose.

That purpose. Could it be? Kyo looked upon the city standing in front of him. Its shape had been solidified now, so that it appeared as a majestic, well-constructed settlement. On top of the walls and, feeling with his mind, within the city, Kyo could see many individuals. Not all of them were alike. Some were fantastical, some were more natural. Again, he had no idea what had produced the bases for those comparisons.

He knew what his purpose was, and he knew the purpose of his companions; it was to teach, to rule, and to watch. Kyo was to watch over this small universe until… what? He didn't know, but if it was until its end, so be it. That's what he would do.

-

It felt as if many years had passed. Kyo had taught, ruled, and watched. He was getting frustrated; all of this great power he wielded and yet none of it was being put to any use. Nothing happened. No one rebelled. Everyone praised his presence. It was simply too peaceful. He talked to his servants, and they all agreed. Of course, being servants, they would, never having any sort of their own individual opinions. Or if they did, they hid such thoughts from his omniscience.

Kyo was sitting on his throne, a regal seat made of gold and scarlet jewels. The beauty of it was meaningless, however, for he had ability to conjure many such thrones from thin air. It made it rather boring. On either side, Anima and Animus sat on their own jade thrones, their regality also an empty aesthetic, wished upon them by doting subjects.

Another such doting subject was entering now, though until recently, within the past few relative months, Kyo did not remembering feeling this citizen's presence among the world he ruled. He chalked it up to the fluid state of the land around him, for it was constantly changing, solidifying, then changing again. It made for some harsh predicaments, but it was all routine, as was everything else. The guest seemed important this time, however, so he sent a servant to notify the cook that a breakfast of some sort might be in order. Hopefully, he wouldn't try waffles again.

What this visitor had with him, though, was anything but routine. Kyo gazed upon the object that was presented to him. It looked to be a small prism, stout and able to be held in one hand. The unfamiliar man knelt before Kyo as he held it out to his ruler. Beside him, he could feel Anima and Animus shift in their thrones. Perhaps they would use their roles as advisors to dissuade him from meeting with this man, but, as their superior, he had a right to do as he pleased.

Kyo stood and waved his hands, "Leave us."

His companions, servants, and guards, at his pressing, all left the throne room. He was not to be disturbed, even though they might feel uneasy. Kyo knew what he was doing, though. He could not feel any weapons on his visitor and any rebellious thoughts would be immediately made known. This man had no such thought. His mind instead was filled with cadences of praise and wonder with no particular target.

"Stand," Kyo commanded, "What it your name?"

The man stood, a peaceful smile on his face, "Serenus, milord."

"And what is this that you have brought to me?"

Serenus held the prism up, "This, one might say, is a gate. It is how I got here."

His response intrigued Kyo; was there more, perhaps, to this limited existence than he knew? He decided to play along with Serenus, "How, daresay, do you define 'here'?"

"Your star, milord. The pocket in space and time in which we currently reside."

So it wasn't his imagination. All those times during which he could sense nothing important within his own world, so instead he turned outward to where the stars should be, he sensed beyond the wall an emptiness, but warmth coming from the direction of each star. The same warmth that came from the sun around which Dream orbited. There was even a small amount of warmth coming from the moon that orbited around Dream. Perhaps it was connected in a way.

If it was, perhaps this man, Serenus, knew how. And so Kyo interrogated, "From which star did you come?"

"Your intuition knows no bounds, milord. I come from a very far star, but one that, in some ways, is closer to yours than most. It is also small like yours, but there is much more freedom in it than this little cage. I come to you with the key, if you will have it." Serenus once again brandished the prism.

Kyo nodded, processing the information. Other stars, far away, but reachable. Could this happen with the help of Serenus? He wanted to know all about this man that he could, though, before he accepted his offering. "Serenus, you come to me with one key, but how are you to return to your home without the aid of one you have for yourself?"

"Milord, this key has lost its shine," he began, "and I have not been able to reawaken it. I am certain you can and, in return for your help, I shall carry you with me to the land where the ore from which these are crafted is plentiful. Then shall you have your own key with which to traverse the stars."

A tempting offer; obviously, none before had given Kyo such a promise of freedom, of being able to leave this small world. Until now, such a thing was impossible, but this visitor from another star was claiming so many things. If indeed Kyo could reawaken the crystal. If that was all it took.

He began to reach for the prism. Kyo's fingers were almost within reach when Animus' voice burst into his head, *Kyo, this man could be dangerous. Do not accept his gift.*

It was Anima's mental voice that responded, *Ah, but Animus, if he were to do so, he would have an infinite plane on which to spread his infinite power. Look how he suffers, boxed into this small cage of a world.*

But, upon examining the crystal closer, it seems to be--
That is enough, Animus. Let Kyo decide what to do.

So Kyo hesitated throughout the short consultation of his friends. The encouragement of Anima and the warnings of Animus. He trusted both equally, but they had rarely disagreed on anything. Why now? Could Anima secretly be wishing to have the kingdom for herself? But that was impossible, for they had a deep connection that allowed them place in each other's thoughts. If she felt in such a way, Kyo would know it.

No, if anything, she knew the freedom he deserved. And wanted. Animus, kind-hearted as he was, knew Kyo was comfortable here in this world, and so encouraged him to stay rooted.

But Kyo longed to go, to be free of his tight shackles. For, try as he might, he could never expand the horizon, never create more to his world than the sun, moon, and Dream. He could stand being here no longer.

Kyo grasped the prism in his hands.

Without a conscious thought, much power passed from his heart into the clear crystal, filling it with a brilliant glow. It was reawakening, but Kyo didn't know what to do next. He looked up to ask Serenus for guidance, but the man had disappeared. Looking back down at the crystal, it had opened, revealing a dark interior. From this interior sprang a stream of darkness, unlike the one from which Kyo had originated. This stream was angry, not passive. It pushed, not flowed.

He watched, horrified, as individual streaks coalesced into monsters, beasts that had never materialized within Dream until now. As more of their kin formed, these beasts turned and ran into the city. The ones that stayed behind rushed at Kyo, trying to claw and tear at him, but no amount of their assaults seemed to touch him. Kyo channeled his Essence and vaporized the demons. He focused on the prism, but the portal within it merely widened.

He felt someone grab his right arm, then his left. Anima and Animus had taken a hold of him and were pulling him away, farther than they had ever gone. So far, the horizon began to shrink, and the world turned into a marble. They were safe, out in the darkness of space where none but them could exist.

That was when Anima turned to him in fury, *What have you done?*

Kyo felt a stab of guilt so deep, he could not bear to reply. Animus spoke for him, *He followed your encouragement and opened a portal to another world. Only this world is pouring contemptible spirits into ours for an unknown purpose. If anything, I shall go and purge them from this world for good.*

Nonsense, Anima spat back, *if you go back down there, you forfeit your right to watch this world.*

How does that make any sense?!

It is because of our interference that this world is now suffering. The best thing we can do is get rid of the source by disconnecting our world from it.

Kyo had an inkling of what she meant, but he still had to ask, *What might that entail?*

It was you who awakened the gate. If... if you were to die, so would the portal.

While he was shocked, of course Kyo had seen it coming. And he did feel a connection to that horrid thing. It was if he were tied to a pole that was covered in rank slime. Once more, a comparison about which he knew nothing. *If that is the only way to undo my mistake, then so be it.*

Animus vigorously shook his head, *Absolutely not. I shall perform the only other course of action, to destroy each and every one of those demons.*

Anima's hair, full of vibrant stars, practically exploded in rage, *Then I shall ensure that you shall stay there forever, to always fight!*

Kyo could hardly watch as Anima plunged her hand into Animus' chest and ripped out his heart -- a crystal that radiated power, small and round in shape -- and pierce her own chest with it, combining her own heart with it. Animus gasped and froze. He began to fall to Dream, unable to move. Kyo was equally paralyzed to act as Anima summoned a preternatural blade and cleaved him in two.

Awake now, half of Kyo examined his appearance. He could feel himself pulling in Essence. Perhaps that was how he had awoken. Now he could see that he had become white, as if his own body had rejected all color. Around him, all he could see was a gray dome. He tried to push out of it, but he could only feel it move with him. He tried to force the Essence he had to collect to force out of it, but he couldn't channel it. It was impossible to him now, so he could only grow in power, but that power couldn't be released.

And he remembered why. Because Anima had tried to kill him. But it hadn't worked. Now Anima was the most powerful being in this small world, but not for much longer. He could still feel his connection to the portal, and, much weaker, the connection to the demons that passed through it.

Using his intact mind, he channeled his hatred, his desire, into his new subjects. Some yielded, some didn't, but that was fine. Eventually, he would control them all. He would destroy Anima for her betrayal. He would have his freedom once he had absorbed her. And he would escape this world, even if he had to destroy it to do so.

While this Kyo, this Reaper, was plotting the destruction of all he knew in favor of the more expansive unknown, the crystal embodying Kyo's heart was stumbled upon by a race of demons untouched by his influence.

And yet further away, in a dense forest of trees tainted by the dark legions that had sprung from the portal, another Kyo was gradually reforming itself. The body.

Kyo had not been killed by Anima, he was merely split. A dark body, a vengeful mind, and a submissive heart.

But now the body, as well as the mind did, remembered.

Chapter 17
Olivia

Olivia had no idea about anything anymore. Kyo had only just shared what he remembered via telepathy and was now facing off against Anima. Knowing what she knew about him now, she could imagine how he felt. Or at least how she would feel in his situation; scared, defiant, and angry all at once. She would be placing the blame on Anima, as well.

The deity in question seemed less brilliant now, more sinister. It was almost as if the collective thoughts of those she had recruited transformed her image into something which they couldn't possibly follow. Anima bore it and dignifiedly spoke, "What I have done is of no matter. It only matters that I am undoing my mistakes to the best of my ability."

"And what exactly are you doing?" Dom shot back.

Though she remained outwardly peaceful, her supernova hair spoke otherwise, "I have gathered you to close the portal, of course. The six of you-"

"Seven," Therin interrupted, "Kyo's with us, no matter what."

Anima gave her a fiery glare, but Therin, defiantly, did not wither, as Olivia imagined she herself would've. When Anima gave up, she resumed her orders, this time with layers of contempt evident in her voice, "The seven of you shall go to where Enrem once was in order to shut the gate that Kyo so foolishly opened. After that, the Reaper should disappear."

"And what happens to Kyo?" Therin asked.

"I suppose, since the Reaper is his mind embodied due to a connection with the portal, he will go into a vegetative state. A coma, if you will."

Kyo glared at her, *That's not what's going to happen. As soon as we close the portal, the Reaper will know exactly where we are. It -- he won't simply vanish. And the connection isn't between the Reaper and the portal, it's between me, him, and our heart.*

He held out the crystal in his hand to identify it as the source of his being. Sira looked at it, taken aback, "That's your heart?!"

Yes. It's what produced Essence when I was whole. My mind stored it and my body manipulated it. That's why-

"Why the Reaper is absorbing everything," Olivia finished. That made enough sense, at least in her head.

Kyo nodded, *Regardless, Anima, we're going to need your help in order to get to Enrem. It's north of here, so there's no way to get there without encountering the Reaper. If we come to meet him, he'll know what's up and the demons will flock around the portal. I don't suppose you could teleport us there?*

"Me? I've come to believe that you are the one with such transcendent powers."

It's true that I can teleport short distances, but I don't think that even with my heart back, I could transfer us all to Enrem.

"I detect passive aggression in your thoughts."

Do you, now?

Olivia couldn't help but smile at the way he was handling Anima, since it was so unheard of. Even though she was nervous about the whole thing, this banter somehow put her at ease, even though Anima's head was likely to blow up. For such a composed deity, she had a hard time concealing her feelings.

She could hear Anima take a long, sharp breath, "Very well, I shall transport you there. I will wait at the edge of the city in order to transport you to a safe distance from the Reaper. I will not touch that profaned place myself, so it is you that will have to close the portal."

Olivia wanted to say that the woman wouldn't touch anything anyway, but the world around her seemed to break into pieces. Suddenly, she couldn't see anymore, she could barely think. Her thoughts were muddied and she could feel something missing. After a brief moment, she realized it was her heartbeat. Then she realized she couldn't move her body. Perhaps she didn't have one at this point.

All Olivia knew was that she was moving incredibly fast. She could feel a glimmer of the world around her as she passed it, but she was struggling to hold herself together, for no doubt she was made of some form of energy that could travel at these speeds.

It only lasted a few moments, but it felt like eternity, as a few moments so often do. When it was over, Olivia felt herself thrust back into the shape she had before the jump, feeling pressed into her body like a sausage. The resulting pain caused her to have a major migraine, which drowned out her rational thought. Soon enough, though, it passed and she was able to look around at where they had been so violently transported.

On one side, vibrant red grass grew long and wavy all the way through forested foothills. The mountains were a long way off, hazy and blue. That was west, then. To the east…

When Olivia turned her head, she almost gasped. The gray wasteland was large and expansive. Dusty remains of the withered grass were carried away in the breeze, creating small clouds of choking filth in the air. Not too far into it, the crumbled walls of a city remained, but only just. The rubble that was left was worn smooth, like stones at the bottom of a river worn away over years of time. Other remnants of structures were scattered past the wall, some slightly more intact than others, but all colorless, as if the life was sucked from the very walls of the houses.

Anima's voice fluttered around her, calling Olivia's attention to her companions, "I will go no further, but straight ahead, you will find the portal. I have no inkling of how to close it, but it is my hope that you will be able to find a way."

For not the first time, Olivia wished that Anima would be more helpful than that, but she supposed that if a gate to another star or whatever opened and demons continuously poured out of it, she would be out of ideas, too. She looked ahead and turned on her eyepiece. There was what looked like a ripple of heat emanating from one of the more intact buildings, no doubt Kyo's old palace.

Olivia turned to Kyo, "You know where it is?"

Within a range of two inches, he turned to Anima, *We'll be back soon.*

She merely nodded in response.

Kyo gestured to Olivia to scout ahead. She flapped out the wings of her poncho that gave her a crow-like appearance. She leaped into a run, taking off at a speed that would blind others, but to her was a lively stroll. Her coat billowed behind her, a dangerous shadow that she knew could rip anything to pieces.

Other than the rippling heat, she saw nothing of interest. Upon scanning the buildings as she ran, nothing of significance seemed to appear. Even as she neared the grand but bleak door that somehow still stood, Olivia observed nothing to raise any alarms.

She touched the door handle in order to open it, but as soon as her fingers met the corroded metal, it withered away into dust. A chain reaction occurred, resulting in an entire half of the door crumbling into nothing. The other half was held by its hinges for a short time, but those quickly broke, leaving the door's half to gravity's pull. As the tall door tumbled to the ground, Olivia sidestepped, but she didn't need to. The edges of the door started to blow away and before it even hit the ground, the entire thing had disappeared.

But that wasn't the important thing.

Behind the door, a river of black spewed out of an ethereal fountain, the small crystal Kyo had described. The eyepiece Olivia wore didn't register any heat signature from the portal itself, but the waves were rippling out from it. She followed the dark fountain, for surely, she would've been able to see the top of it spewing out above the walls of the worn palace. However, as she tracked the stream, she found it harder and harder to see, for it all but disappeared. At the end of it, small heat differences randomly burst from it, scattering in all directions at different speeds. The demons. If they cut off this flow, it would be impossible for any more to form. Whether they would all die at once after their connection to their home world was severed was left to be discovered.

Olivia signaled Kyo via telepathy, *It's clear, there's no ambush.*
Roger. We'll be there soon.

All Olivia had to do was wait for them to get there. That wasn't so hard. She sat down roughly on the soft ground, causing a cloud of dust to erupt and get in her nose. When she breathed in, she had to sneeze hard. The jolt from the sneeze scattered more dust. Before she could take another clogged breath, she pulled her poncho over her nose, filtering the air before it reached her nostrils.

Like this, her breathing and the world quiet, she had time to think and to listen. To think about how to close the portal and to listen to… the portal. It made a whispering sound, alike to a fountain, as if that was what it had decided to mimic upon opening. It flowed back and forth in random patterns, which she came to understand were the same patterns that the demon spawning followed.

Olivia closed her eyes; the whispering was somewhat calming, for whatever reason. With her other senses shut out, she was able to listen to it more closely. The actual sound of it was something like sandpaper softly shifting over a smooth board of wood, but each whisper seemed… uniquely shaped. She started to strain her ears. Sure enough, she began to hear words, a chant nearly inaudible. It had rhythm, rhyme, but it wasn't any sort of language she could recognize.

Olivia listened to it harder and started to feel the rest of the world slip away. It became harder to think, harder to feel the many layers of dust beneath her. Eventually, all she was aware of was the whispering. The endless, incessant whispering.

Then someone shook her. Olivia's eyes flew open and she was back where she was before. The destroyed throne room loomed around her, the fountain of darkness still flowing upward. Ryan stood over her, a worried look on his face.

She shook her head vigorously, "Sorry. Don't listen to that thing; it'll put you under some form of hypnosis."

Sira folded her arms. "Or you're just tired," she suggested.

She rolled her eyes and stood up, "You're right; Anima kinda woke us up pretty abruptly."

Whatever, let's figure out how to close this thing. Kyo walked up to the portal, looking at it from all angles, even below.

"Anything useful?" Dom asked.

Hardly. This thing is basically impossible to figure out. He stuck his hand into the dark stream. It flowed around his fingers, unperturbed, just like water. Kyo lowered his hand to the opening of the portal, as if to put it through. There was a loud sizzling sound and the rank smell of burning flesh. Kyo quickly withdrew his hand and showed the rest of them the exposed bone and tissue, the skin having melted right off his hand. *It's one way, apparently.* He took the crystal in his other hand and waved it over the palm of his wounded hand, instantly repairing it. Olivia did her best not to throw up.

Dom, somehow unfazed, made another inquiry, "How did you try to close it in the first place?"

I tried destroying the crystal directly, but that only made the portal larger.

"Then it's obvious; we merely have to take the Essence that it's using to keep the portal open."

Ryan looked worried, "Would that even be possible?"

Sure, but it would be hard to actually store it somewhere. I'm not entirely sure how much it has, but it's got to be a lot, since it took it from me when I was whole.

Therin rubbed her hands together, "Then how do we get started?"

I don't know, place a hand on it and pull with your mind? Usually things like this are pretty straightforward.

"That's it?" She adopted a dramatically disappointed face, "I was thinking we'd have to perform some complicated ritual or something."

Why would that be?

"This is a dream, right? You would think a dream wouldn't be straightforward."

If it's a dream, whose dream is it? I've been here for what's felt like decades. Centuries, even.

No one had an answer. Then Aly spoke up, "A friend of mine's been having a dream like this recently. At least, with red grass and stuff."

Olivia blinked. That's right, Aly was still here. She had nearly forgotten, since she'd been so quiet since Kyo had revealed his past. But now she said she might know something about this world? Olivia was curious, "What friend?"

"His name's..." Aly hesitated, "Well, he's Zach."

Olivia gasped and she could hear almost everyone else gasp, as well. The only ones who didn't were Kyo and Dom, the latter of whom looked confused as he asked, "Who's Zach?"

Almost simultaneously, Olivia, Therin, Ryan, Aly, and Sira replied, "A friend."

But why would your friend be having this dream? Could Anima have been looking at him as a potential candidate?

Aly nodded, "That could be. After all, he's only seventeen, so he couldn't have been alive to dream the whole world up."

Anyway, we're digressing too far. Let's pull this thing apart.

Almost in response, the portal screamed. A horrible, high-pitched scream much like the Reaper.

"Now we're in for it," Olivia yelled over the portal.

Dom gestured for them to gather around, "Let's go!"

Olivia took her place on one side of the portal and placed her hand on it. She could feel it pulling at her Essence, but she stubbornly refused, holding her own power back. More than that, though, she pulled at the Essence she felt in the prism. It came not slowly, like she thought, but all at once, an unrelenting torrent just like the fountain bursting out of the portal.

The Essence flowed through her arm and into her heart. She could feel all of it spreading out through her entire body, trying to rip her apart from the inside out. Olivia tried, gently, to let it out. Instead of obeying her wishes, however, the forceful… force… burst out of her mouth, its flames reaching for the sky. It burned her entire being and she had to give up.

Olivia's hand left the prism and the surplus flow stopped. The remaining Essence in her flowed out, leaving just her life force and the Essence she had herself. Every muscle in her body ached. It was a horrible sensation, but anything was preferable to the overwhelming fire of the gate's Essence.

She blinked the tears out of her eyes and found that she had collapsed. Olivia was looking up at the portal now, which was swiftly closing. Everybody else was on the ground, though, perhaps just as overwhelmed as she had been by the huge amount of power within the prism.

Well, everyone except Kyo.

He was still standing, his hand still on the portal. Olivia could actually see the ribbons of Essence that were flowing up his arm, around his body, and into his skin. With each converging ribbon, his flesh brightened until he was glowing almost as much as he had before against the Reaper. Kyo's head twitched and his body began to morph strangely. Scales sprouted on his arms and faces, his fingers elongating into claws. His gritted teeth became fangs and his eyes shone gold. His black shirt seemed to unfold, but it wasn't his shirt, it was a pair of enormous reptilian wings. It was as if Kyo had turned into a dragon, but kept his human shape.

Gradually, though, the mutations receded, as did the glow. The ribbons became fewer and farther between and the portal was almost closed now. As soon as Kyo returned to his normal self, the portal closed, cutting off the dark fountain. The prism, no longer suspended in midair, fell to the ground and shattered. Kyo also fell, just to his knees, but he was clearly exhausted. Olivia would be, too, if she had had to absorb a portal's Essence and be forcibly transfigured for a brief time.

Therin sat up, "Well, that was surprising."

Kyo huffed almost audibly, *I don't know what happened, personally, but I found it surprising, too.*

Olivia was blinded by a sudden flash of light. When she had blinked it away, she stood up and looked around for the source, as the others were doing. She ran out of the open doorway and whipped her head around. Her eyes fixated on it. From the direction they had come, the Reaper was bearing down upon them.

Olivia pointed at it and spoke just loud enough for everyone to hear, "Not as surprising as that."

Chapter 18
Sira

Why did everything they ended up doing have to be running? Sira felt like she had lost more weight in these past few days than she cared about. But considering it wasn't her real body, it might've just been her imagining things. Regardless of whether or not she had lost weight, Sira and her friends were now running from the Reaper, which had just absorbed Anima.

"Sorry!" Aly apologized.

"For what, exactly?" Sira asked.

"I foreshadowed this. Dom told me not to."

She rolled her eyes, "Don't worry, I'm sure it couldn't have been avoided, foreshadowing or not."

The younger girl simply nodded and continued to sprint. Sira turned away from the conversation as well and, as she was running, began to think. After the Reaper had absorbed Animus, it had been able to fly. Since it had now absorbed Anima, what might happen--

A massive gray dome popped into existence twenty feet ahead of them. Oh, that's what. Sira ground to a halt, her heels scattering dust into the air. Through the cloud behind her, she could see the original gray dome, smaller than before. Glancing back and forth, she saw that the domes were of the same size. Great, so the Reaper now had the ability to perform mitosis.

Kyo, she noticed, wasn't busy comparing sizes, but was instead summoning his own pearly white sphere from his heart, which expanded to encompass the seven of them. As soon as it was formed, he resumed running, taking the barrier with him. The Reaper in front of them literally screeched to a halt, hissing against Kyo's barrier and letting off steam. Sira decided it was best to follow closely.

They had to head around it, which led them through a maze of dilapidated buildings that crumbled under their feet. Sira did her best to run ahead with Therin to break down any obstructive walls. Several times, they blasted through weakened bricks, Therin perforating them from a distance with her spear and Sira ramming them with her bladed armor.

As a result, they were able to make steady progress around the new Reaper dome, which was continuously being pushed back by Kyo's barrier. Sira's shoes crunched on new terrain and she looked down to see flattened, brittle grass. They were outside what used to be the city now, and the grass here, contrary to the usually vibrant red, was blackened and crumbled loudly beneath each hurried step.

Sira looked back up and continued running, since that was all they could ever do. They began to come around the widest part of Reaper number two when Sira was encouraged by how easy the escape was going to be, compared to the last couple ones.

She spoke too soon. Immediately after the thought crossed her mind, two more domes appeared around them, blocking their escape further. Sira stopped dead in her tracks and the rest of them did, too. Therin, however, kept running, seemingly unaware of the change in the situation. Sira glanced around and saw that one of the domes was closing in on the point that Therin would exit the safe zone. Desperately, in order to prevent the girl from reaching the border that was so close now, Sira yelled, "Therin, stop!"

First her wolf ears swiveled to pick up the sound, then she turned, sliding across the weak grass as she tried to halt. The border seemed to close the distance on its own, with Therin looking as if she were standing still, since the landscape was so unchanging. Gradually, the grass stopped her. But one hand slipped out of the barrier, breaching the wall of protective light. At the same time, the oncoming dome became tangent at exactly the point where Therin's hand breached the unsheltered air.

Her scream was horrifying, layers of pain rang out from her vocal cords, tearing at them and the air. Kyo's mental scream was equally loud, *Therin!*

Between the two, both Sira's ears and brain hurt, causing her to shut out her vision. It didn't help much. When she opened her eyes again, she saw that the boundary hadn't moved, but Kyo was tearing Therin away from the Reaper and Ryan was sprinting to help. Sira, despite her migraine, ran as fast as she could to them, as well.

When she caught up, she gasped when she saw Therin. The girl's skin was white and she was shivering. The hand that had been touched by the Reaper was rotting away, crumbling into dust until it began to spread slowly up the rest of her arm. Kyo was hugging her close, trying to keep her hoodie around her to keep her warm. She whispered through blue lips, "It's so cold."

Ryan rubbed her good hand, tears in his eyes, "We'll get you warm, right, Kyo?"

Sira looked at him. He was crying, too. His eyes were full of... something. Confidence? No, it was definitely determination. He met Sira's eyes, those deep black eyes reassuring and bolstering at the same time. *Don't worry, it's only her life force being eaten.*

Sira's heart went heavy, "I assume since you can be sarcastic, you already have a solution?"

Of course.

Ryan touched his arm, "Please."

I just have to give her some of mine.

"What?!" Dom gasped.

Olivia and Aly had just caught up, as well. Olivia asked concernedly, "But won't you die?"

He shook his head. *Don't worry, I've got plenty. And besides,* he held out his hand and the crystal, his heart, flew into it, *this'll always make more.*

Therin gasped and reached her hand up to touch his face, "You don't... have to. I'll just warm myself... up with some fire." She was speaking with a quivering voice from the cold of having her life drained away. Sira had a hard time not retching at the horror of it all.

In response, Kyo grabbed her hand tightly, *You barely have the strength to breathe, let alone light a fire.*

She pulled her hand free and lightly punched him, "Stop doubting me."

Stop wasting my time so I can save you.

"I told you... I'm... fi..." Her voice trailed off as her eyes rolled back in her head.

When she went limp, Ryan practically screamed, "Save her!"

Kyo didn't say anything, he merely touched his crystal to Therin's chest and narrowed his eyes in concentration. Webs of Essence enveloped her from head to toe. Where her decayed arm had been, a matrix of Essence strands wove themselves together in the shape of the lost limb, solidifying into a new appendage. As the magic folded into Therin, the protective dome around them narrowed considerably, but it was still spacious.

When the Essence faded, Therin's eyes didn't open. Ryan's tears started flowing again, "Did it work?"

Kyo smiled, *Of course it worked; she's just not opening her eyes in order to put another cliché in this story.*

Therin coughed and sputtered, "What happened?"

He lightly punched her, *Don't pretend. You did that on purpose.*

"Okay, so I did. But did you have to spoil it?"

Sira interrupted, "So you're feeling better?"

She nodded and sat up shakily, but on her own. Therin held out her restored arm and snapped her fingers, causing a small flame to flicker above them. She sighed with content and dropped her arm. She turned to Kyo and tackled him with a hug, which he immediately returned, both of them crying. Sira could barely hear her whisper, "Thank you."

After a little bit, they pushed away from each other and Therin turned to hug Ryan, though not as forcefully. Sira watched as the younger girl started to smile again and poke and prod her twin brother as if nothing had happened. As if she hadn't been on the brink of death just a moment ago. How she could turn around so quickly was something Sira couldn't understand, for she was still in shock.

Dom cleared his throat, "Um, I hate to interrupt."

Sira looked up at him, his head backdropped by a gray sky. Wait, but wasn't it the middle of the day? She stood up and looked around, noticing now that gray spheres surrounded them, encompassing their refuge on all sides, not leaving so much as an inch of room. They were above them, too, eclipsing the sky like a canopy of death. She whipped around to Kyo, who was helping Therin stand up, "Can you get us out of here?"

I've been trying to push against them for the past couple of minutes, but I can't make any ground. If I tried to teleport, well, I could only take one or two of you at a time and that would require dropping the barrier. Since these Reapers are so small, they're bound to be much faster. There's no way I can get us out feasibly.

Sira sighed in defeat. She could feel her body deflate as she came to grips with the situation. Wherever they went, the shell of Reapers would no doubt follow, so there was no way for them to get anywhere without destroying what they were trying to get. That is, if they could somehow see where they were going. There was also no way to get more resources and if they tried to dig down, no doubt the Reapers would just follow them above the ground.

She heard a snap. She turned to see Dom, his eyes alight with an idea, "What if you didn't try to push away the Reaper?"

Kyo tilted his head, evidently curious, *What do you mean?*

As Dom explained his idea only to the other characters and not to the readers, so as not to bore them, Sira felt hope rising in her. Especially when Kyo nodded, *It could work. It's not like we have any other options.*

"So, go on, do it." She urged him.

Kyo closed his eyes and held up his crystal, which began to glow again. The amount of Essence in the air pounded around inside their barrier, giving Sira another migraine. When the pressure became almost impossible to bear, the barrier shattered and the Reaper began to close in on them. Sira ducked and closed her eyes, waiting for the worst, since the plan had very obviously failed.

It never came.

When she opened her eyes, each separate Reaper was encompassed in a protective barrier turned cage, their gray forced to shimmer with pearly resonance. She could almost feel the hatred emanating from the many assailants as they were forced into the same space. Kyo visibly began to sweat with the effort of shifting the barriers to make the Reaper coalesce back into its singular form. The spheres began to join together, reluctantly obeying the pressing of the no doubt painful cage that was impelling them into each other.

Sira watched as the Reaper grew larger and larger with each rejoined sphere, it's gray dome still ensnared by Kyo's barrier. At last, it was done, the Reaper held in front of them, looming, but no longer piercing their hearts with fear. She heard it screech and saw why; a tunnel was being formed into it by the barrier, leading into the belly of the beast.

Sira looked over at Kyo, who was starting to walk towards the tunnel. Therin grabbed his hand, stopping him. He turned back to her and took her hands in his. Sira couldn't hear anything pass between them, but they were undoubtedly having a silent conversation, for Therin's eyes began to well up in response to something only she was able to hear. She let go of his hands.

Just as Kyo was turning back to the Reaper, he was caught by another hand, this one belonging to Aly. Sira blinked, curious as to why she of all people would stop him.

The girl stammered as she spoke, but it was plain what she was saying, "You don't have to."

Yes, I do.

"No, you don't! I barely know you, but I know you shouldn't just throw your life away because you have to stop that thing forever!"

Sira was taken aback. It was true that Aly had only just gotten here, but she apparently had an understanding of what Kyo was doing that Sira didn't have. In her ignorance, she just had to ask, "What are you planning to do?"

Therin was the one who responded, "He needs to go in there and... end the Reaper."

"But he can't! He can't, he just can't!" Aly yelled in protest.

Kyo put his hands on her shoulders, *He can and he will. Aly, I know I remind you of someone, but I'm not them. If you lose me, it'll be like losing a bad picture you never wanted taken.*

That confused Sira. Kyo reminded Aly of somebody in the real world? How could that be? But then again, it wasn't really all that far-fetched; in the couple of days that she'd known him, Sira had noticed some of his mannerisms that were similar to... someone. She could never quite place whom. She'd never noticed until now, when Aly called it out.

Ryan stepped toward him, "And what about you?"

"Yeah," Olivia agreed, "what happens to you when your mind dies?"

Kyo shrugged in response, *It's as Anima said; if I survive, it'll be as a vegetable, unable to walk or talk or do anything, really. But that way, Dream is safe and you're safe. Now, if you'd stop bothering me, I need to walk into a menacing embodiment of my brain in order to save your guys' lives.*

Sira couldn't just watch him go without putting in her two cents, "What'll it prove?"

He turned to her, his face blank as he spoke into her mind, *Prove? I wasn't thinking of proving anything.*

"Except how little you value your life, apparently."

Kyo visibly sighed through his nose, *I suppose that's one way of looking at things.* He turned to the Reaper and began walking, not looking back.

"What's the other?" Sira asked.

Without stopping, he responded, *That I value your lives much more than I do mine.*

She could barely take it. Tears escaped her eyes. She tried to blink them away and they blurred her vision. When she had cleared them enough, the Reaper had closed its dome behind Kyo, who was now inside.

Sira saw Therin collapse to the ground, her face buried in her hands and her shoulders shaking with sobs. Ryan knelt next to her to comfort her, rubbing her bare shoulder, the hoodie having slipped off one side.

They didn't have much time to grieve, though, for Sira heard the brittle crunch of grass, but much more constant and distant that it had been under her own feet. She looked behind her, back to the city. On the other side of the dusty ruins, she could see black legions of demons, all approaching at the same pace towards the Reaper's dome. Looks like Kyo wasn't the only one with something about which to worry.

She formed knives from the water that she felt in the air, ones that could both reliably slice and be thrown. Sira glanced back at the others. Therin was just getting up on her feet, but Ryan, Olivia, Dom, they were all more or less ready to fight until the Reaper was destroyed. Sira had no idea if the barrier could be sabotaged from the outside, but at all costs, she felt like she had to defend it, especially if what Kyo thought would happen did. She didn't want his body dying after all that hard work to lose his own mind.

Chapter 19
Kyo

A bubble within a bubble within a bubble. When he thought about it, if it wasn't so scary, the way he was infiltrating the Reaper's dome was kind of amusing, since it produced an imagery that reinforced the... oh, whatever, Kyo wasn't interested in all that. Not at the moment, anyway. Right now, he was interested in keeping both his inner bubble and the outer bubble in place in order to keep the Reaper out and in respectively. Oh great, now it was complicated. He kept walking regardless.

Beneath his feet, the grass was much more drained than outside, crumbling to the very wind brushed up by his steps. It was strange. As he went deeper, it became easier to progress, to hold out the Reaper, contrary to how he thought it would go. He expected he would've had to push for every inch of ground, but instead, it was as if he was being ushered along a line, one in which everyone else had to wait, but he could move right along to the front.

What was it with these comparisons? Kyo didn't know what lines were, since even the subjects that had come to see him before he was split never had to wait in one. Every time he came up with an analogy he didn't fully understand, it confused him. It was almost like... trying to remember a dream that he had last night, but not being able to.

Strange, isn't it?

The voice seemed to come from everywhere, scaring Kyo to death. He looked around, but he already knew the source. Ahead, the darker dome was the same size as it had been that first day that they had encountered the Reaper closely.

Of course I can speak to you; now that you're within my own rudimentary body, speaking to your rudimentary mind is a simple task.

Kyo responded, *I can only imagine.*

Ah, telepathy. I didn't think you'd still have that after Anima killed us.

I have friends.

Kyo could almost hear the Reaper laugh, *Alas, so you did. But now you are here, without them. Please, come closer.*

What little pressure was left on Kyo's barrier relaxed. If he didn't know better, he would release it, leaving himself unsheltered within the Reaper. However, then he would be unable to get what he wanted. Kyo walked forward, reaching the darker gray dome. Hesitantly, he put a hand out to touch it. It passed right through with no trouble at all. Kyo stepped into it.

Within was a bright small world, completely saturated with color. The grass beneath was a fuller red than Kyo had seen outside. A strange assortment of objects was scattered about, littering the ground with no rhyme or reason to their piling. In the midst of them sat a small figure, turned away from Kyo.

"Like them?"

Kyo didn't respond. He didn't recognize any of the objects, so he had no opinion on them. Besides, they were too cluttered for his taste. However, he did identify the cloak that the figure wore. The shape of it, anyway. The main color was the original white, but now there were streams of deep red decorating it with black trim on the sleeves. The figure -- no, the Reaper stood up, revealing the blood red leggings he wore to match his cloak. He turned to face Kyo, revealing the kitsune mask that he was wearing. "It's good to meet you at long last."

I'd return the sentiment, but you've tried to kill me a lot.

"But isn't that what you're here to do? To kill me?"

When Kyo didn't respond, the Reaper took off his mask, revealing a face identical to Kyo's. However, the color was very different from his; the hair was white, matching the mask; when he smiled wide, hints of his blood red mouth stood out against his shining teeth; and most disturbing of all, his eyes were all white, no pupils or irises. "I thought you'd at least appreciate my outfit. I realized I should clothe myself once I figured out what you wanted to try."

How nice, you're almost civilized. Where'd you get the threads? Since you wanted me to ask.

The Reaper gestured to the piles of stuff around him, "Some of the objects I absorb are just too good to destroy. So, I formed a collection. Most of these things are just some sentimental memorabilia from the cities I've razed, like this little trinket," he picked up a glass pair of wings, "This belonged to some sort of ultimate pixie or whatever. But I digress," he threw the glass wings behind him, effectively shattering them carelessly, "when I reaped Anima and Animus, well, I figured something a bit more personal was in order."

Kyo smiled, despite how unnerved he was to be talking to himself in such a situation, *You seem to be in a talkative mood.*

"Well, when you can only talk to demons for five relative years -- and they never talk back, mind you -- you tend to get kind of lonely."

It's taken you five years to get to this point? How pitiful.

"You're one to talk. You're just a body that formed its own mind. That took you five years. The only thing you had on me is that heart there. But now I have two hearts, one from Anima and one from Animus. Though I kind of got a two-for-one deal when I reaped her and got both."

In order to stall further -- though for what he was stalling, he had no idea -- Kyo asked, *I'm curious; when you… reaped Animus, you were able to fly, but when you absorbed Anima, you began to divide yourself. It's strange, since those were each the powers the other used.*

"It did surprise me, but I've found you shouldn't be in this world. Ever since that portal opened, things have never been straight."

As I recall, things weren't straight in the first place.

"Did you just assume my gender?" The Reaper exclaimed in mocking hurt.

This world was created haphazardly. Or didn't you notice, having eaten half of it without being able to see?

"Now that's hurtful; you're just mad because I look different. But I guess you're right. That's why I've been trying to destroy it, so that I can escape." He bent down to pick something up. He held it out for Kyo to see. It was the crystal that had opened the portal.

I thought--

"What, you thought that because you had closed it that you'd gotten rid of it forever? You really are helpless without your real mind. I can't imagine how you managed to get this far without me. Actually, against me, since I am your missing mind. Oh, wait, I know. It's because it was all part of my plan."

Kyo's eyes widened, *It was?*

"Of course not," the Reaper laughed, "but it sure seems like it, doesn't it?"

He went silent again, not wanting another response to be turned into a jibe from himself. Kyo couldn't process all of this at once, but he knew he didn't have to, since all he had to do was destroy his mind.

"I suppose if you're gonna kill me, you better get on with it."

Why are you not scared?

"Oh, you noticed. Gosh, I really should be more careful about my feelings," the Reaper's voice was layered with sarcasm. A lot of it.

Trying to seem confident, Kyo pointed the crystal at him, *Why are you not scared?* He repeated.

"Hmm. Perhaps it has something to do with the fact that you can't kill me."

I can very well kill you. Right here, right now.

The Reaper pretended to think about it, "I don't see how. What's your method?"

Kyo blinked, realizing he hadn't thought it through. If he merely blasted the Reaper, that would merely make him stronger.

"And if you tried to tear me apart like the portal, I would simply split again, perhaps recreating Anima and Animus. But I'd still be here and you guys'd still be trapped."

Get out of my head, Kyo demanded.

"I'm not in your head, I am your head. I don't know how many times I have to say it. I am you, just better at thinking." The Reaper bragged.

At least I'm better-looking.

"What are you, five? Oh, and Therin's life force was very tasty. A shame you interrupted my meal."

You're disgusting.

"You're the one in love with her," he accused Kyo, "And now you've gone and tied yourself together with her. How sly of you. You really should be arrested."

At having his feelings called out, Kyo shrunk a bit. He could barely think as he stood in defiance, *I have no idea what you're talking about.*

"We had a name before we were split. It wasn't Kyo, it wasn't the Reaper. I can't remember what it was, but I imagine I'll remember once I reunite with you."

Now Kyo had a headache, *Now I really don't know what you're talking about.*

"It's 'about what you're talking', but whatever. Let's just examine the major players, shall we? Anima, the feminine impulses in a man. Animus, the masculine in a woman. Even your name is a pitiful attempt at symbolism."

What do you mean? The way the Reaper was talking, always quickly, with an intelligent air, even when he wasn't being formal, it confused Kyo even more than the subject matter.

"I don't know much Japanese, but I do know that 'Kyo' just happens to mean 'unity'. It seems as if your self-chosen name was chosen by someone else. Someone who wanted us to be reunited," he concluded.

Kyo could hardly grasp it, *But who? Who would do that?*

"It doesn't matter. The only thing that does is that you're here and I'm here. Oh yeah, and I have to power to strip your will from that body and claim it for myself."

He stepped back, pointing the crystal at the Reaper once again, *You can't. You won't.*

"Why? Because you have friends? Because you've been stalling this whole time and some *deus ex machina* is going to drop in and save you all? No, I don't think so. Since you've so clearly forgotten, I'm your mind. I've calculated every outcome that you could possibly comprehend. Not one of them ends with you winning."

The Reaper stepped closer, unflinching against the crystal pointed at him. With each step, he let out another menacing word, "I. Will. Not. Let. You. Have. That. Body."

Kyo kept the crystal pointed at the Reaper, but it was in vain. The Reaper simply walked into it, the crystal glowing as it entered his chest, as if it belonged there the whole time. Kyo looked into the Reaper's blank eyes. Slowly, pupils and irises began to form, the glazed eyes creepily staring back at him. The Reaper raised up one hand and touch Kyo's forehead. His head exploded in pain. He heard a barely audible "Thanks" before losing all his senses.

Chapter 20
Finale

Aly

Aly waved her scythe around, tearing through yet another wave of demons. She didn't care about it being hard to form, she just wanted to wield its glorious pink blade. She didn't have a HappyMo or anything that could summon it for her, so she'd used the time she'd had to form it out of the ground, pliable as it was. Now she was slicing through the army of demons like they were made of paper. It was good fun and took her mind off of things.

Understanding what her goal was, defense of the dome, however contrary it felt, was important to her, since it gave her a sense of purpose. Aly thought about Kyo in there, all alone and probably having his own battle. He'd better be all right. If he wasn't... what? He was right, she barely knew him. So why did she feel like she had such a connection with him? Whenever he spoke with telepathy, his inner voice was weird, but it always reminded her of... no, but that couldn't be. He was still awake and moving even before Aly fell asleep.

Blinking out of her reverie, Aly deflected an axe from one of the minotaur demons, spinning closer to the beast and slicing through it with the edge of her weapon. She found it fascinating that instead of falling to the ground and spouting blood, they simply faded into darkness. To her, it was a little disappointing, since she had seen more than her fair share of gory video games or anime, so this fantasy violence was really nothing.

Aly found herself leaping around with her scythe, spinning and flipping just like her fanime character, Mii-chan would. Aly had never been athletic, but it helped to use wind to her advantage. And since her weapon was already formed...

"Transform!" She yelled. Aly didn't care if she sounded cringy; she was having fun and she wanted guns. She broke her scythe in the middle of the pole and each half of it morphed into a glowing, pink pistol. They were really flashy, casting pink and purple sparkles over the surrounding beasts. Aly let loose, blasting round after round of ethereal ammunition into her audience. Crowd. Mob? What was a good word for a waiting group of monsters? Ugh, she was no good at narrating.

The field around her was pretty clear, so she heard the loud shattering noise from behind her. That was weird. Aly was pretty sure the only thing behind her was the… oh. She had turned to see what it was and watched as the shards of what was once the Reaper clattered down like a broken window, surrounding a small, white-robed figure in the middle.

Ryan

Another one bit the dust, jammed in the jaw by an ash-covered rock spire. Ryan felt as if every monster around him was targeting him. He supposed they were, since they probably chose their target based on smell. Not that he was calling himself smelly, but he felt pretty much alone, isolated as he was within this mob, so it was probably a lot easier for them to mob him rather than go off in search of another target.

Happily, though, Ryan obliged the demons scrambling for their taste of his sword. The fighting style he'd created around it required a lot of twisting and turning, so he aided it, blasting jets of wind from his free hand or rooting his foot in the epicenter of an earthen whirlpool. With the combination of his ferocious fighting methods and his manipulation of the ground, huge clouds of dust were thrown up, clogging the air around him.

And that worked to his advantage. Even as he was focusing on destroying immediate threats, Ryan was able to feel new ones that entered his shroud of dust. These demons, if he could spare the concentration, were immediately speared with rocks from below, destroyed by a thrown projectile, or simply choked when the cloud suddenly collapsed around them.

Eventually, they seemed to get the idea, for none were now entering Ryan's area. So, instead of wait for more, he condensed the surrounding cloud into manipulatable threads of earth, swirling around him like tentacles. With the obstruction gone, he was able to see his surroundings; countless demons crowded in specific locations, including his. Thankfully, the number was six, which meant none of his friends had fallen yet. And still, they were somehow holding the horde back from the Reaper.

Ryan dodged an arrow and looked at its source. A Kiyeng, screaming bloody murder. Guess it wasn't time to hesitate. He leapt toward the Kiyeng, his earth tentacles sprawling out behind him, rapidly stabbing other side targets. He saw the Kiyeng's eyes widen and imagined that he looked like something out of a creepypasta.

The rest of the demons' terror was clear as Ryan stabbed the Kiyeng with his sword, his earthen extensions still flailing about, not letting a single opponent draw near. In his opinion, it was quite an effective method of defense, as well as offense, for now he would only have to worry much about projectiles, which were easily deflectable, considering the lack of ability among Ryan's enemies. Heck, there were even some stupid enough to wade into his area of effect and get struck down by a stream of dirt. It was quite amusing to see their undignified faces as they disintegrated.

What wasn't amusing was the sound of a thousand windows breaking. He couldn't see around the horde, but he could see above some of their heads. Enough to realize that the sky was now uninterrupted by an arching dome.

Dom

Dom wanted to narrate a little bit further than the breaking of the Reaper. He thought it was kind of fair, considering he was the closest when it happened. His ears still rang of the earth-shaking noise of it, in fact. His head felt rattled and his vision was blurred. Then he realized he was on the ground, surrounded by demons.

He sprang to his feet, a little unsteadily. He stumbled, but realized the demons weren't looking at him, they were gazing in the direction the Reaper was. He too turned to see the cause of the shatter. He wondered if Kyo had finished off the entity so quickly. If he had, what was he like now? Through the tangle of complicated shapes of demons, he couldn't see, so he ascended.

Dom didn't like what he saw. In the middle of a circle of lush red grass, a figure was crouching on the ground. He was clothed in a white robe, blemished by red. He wore red pants and his feet were bare. He raised his head covered in wild brown hair, his back to

Dom. Eerily, he stood and turned to look directly up at Dom, his eyes blue and piercing, a maniacal smile breaching his pale face. He felt a shiver run down his spine.

Looking at him, Dom knew this wasn't Kyo. It was obvious as soon as he saw the clothes. This was undoubtedly the Reaper, and Dom could feel his well of immense power. Except now it was unrestricted. Now he had the ability to unleash it upon everything he saw.

The Reaper's mouth moved and Dom heard his voice inside his head, even though from this distance, hearing him should've been impossible, "What's the matter, Dom? Got a problem with how I look?"

That was even creepier; how could the Reaper possibly know what Dom thought?

"Oh, it's simple, really. I know you and how you think. I've known you for a while, actually. We're best friends, in fact."

Nothing about this thing was familiar. His speech didn't even carry any mannerisms from Kyo. "How can you possibly be my friend?"

Dom? Olivia spoke into his head, *Are you getting stuff from the Reaper too?*

I am. Sira replied.

Aly used her telepathy as well, *Something weird's going on.*

What did he say to you guys? Dom asked.

Sira spoke up, *That I'm his friend.*

The others voiced their agreement. Apparently, they had all heard the same thing. *Does he sound familiar to you at all?*

Their silence was the only answer Dom needed. He was the only one who didn't know this monster. He could take comfort in that, for it meant that he was the only one who wasn't really known by the Reaper, for whatever reason.

The Reaper levitated, looking down and around at his audience, his worshippers, his demons. "A pitiful bunch, this one. They hardly have minds of their own. Such a shame, really. I'm just glad they came around to my point of view."

Dom feel a thousand pairs of eyes shift to him. He looked at the Reaper, who appeared tantalized by the tension in the air. The tension he himself carried, an eager desire to destroy the world beneath him. The tension Dom felt, waiting for the word that would put him in hideous danger. The demons below him, struggling to remain still until their command came.

All that tension was released when the Reaper spoke, "Get them."

Sira

There was no helping it. Sira had to jump above the demons attempting to tear her apart. Were it not for their projectiles, she'd completely ignore them. However, each icy platform she summoned, she ensured was spiked with long, sharp icicles that would pierce her enemies below as she ascended. The Reaper just got on her nerves so much, she couldn't bear to turn her full attention to his lackeys. Even as she was casting about her long, icy knives, she wasn't particularly concerned with her targets.

After all she'd been through with her friends and with Kyo, to have his life thrown away just like that was preposterous. Sira could feel the heat of anger rising in her chest, burning up her heart and bringing blush to her face.

The Reaper was on the same level as her, above everything. The way he watched everything aloof like that got on her nerves, too. What, did he plan to destroy everything no matter the outcome? At the rate his so-called forces were disappearing, he'd have to be pretty confident in his own abilities to allow such destruction to happen. That snide little son of an eight-ball.

Sira threw a knife at him, knowing it wouldn't do any damage. Just as she thought, the Reaper caught it by the point of the blade and it instantly melted. Perfect, now she had a gauge of his power. Basically, limitless. No big deal. Sira hadn't ever dealt with limitless opponents before, but it couldn't be much worse than the limited ones.

The Reaper's voice resonated even more strongly than Anima's had, "You're brave."

Rushing at him, throwing more ice knives, Sira replied, "And you're fat."

"Actually, technically, no. The robe's just large." He caught another knife, "I'd appreciate it if you'd stop throwing snowflakes at me."

She drew a halo of water from the air, "They're not really shaped like snowflakes, you know."

"They are at a microscopic level."

Not wanting to argue about fractals further, Sira threw gushes of water from her halo, simultaneously replenishing it. When the torrents touched him, they evaporated immediately, casting a cloud of steam into the air. She stayed in motion, suspicious of his casual attitude. Her platform moved in an arc around where the Reaper was while Sira disguised her movements by casting water from where she used to be.

Despite her efforts, the Reaper seemed to materialize out of the steam, headed straight for her. Sira threw up her hands, summoning a shield formed out of heavy-flowing water, enough to deflect a weapon. Some sort of scythe, oddly shaped, was turned aside by the water flow. The Reaper hardly reacted, but instead just floated there, his feet hanging below him.

"How come you're so scared?" He asked, that sickening smile spreading across his face again.

Sira didn't feel like replying verbally.

"Is it the scythe? I can make it something different if you want." He floated back a bit and held out the scythe, letting it float in front of his outstretched hand. It shifted into a claymore, then an axe, then some sort of gun sword like in video games. None of them were more comforting when the weapon finally disappeared completely. But for some reason, the Reaper just smiled wider, "Or maybe the reason you're afraid is because you know that I'm able to get through that lousy shield of yours. All I need to do…"

Sira began to panic as the Reaper reached out his hand to touch her vortex of water. With the lightest of touches, his finger punctured through it, pouring steam into her refuge, making it hotter and harder to breathe.

Gosh, that was annoying. Of course she would be done in by the Reaper, who was so hot, ice melted and water evaporated on contact. Oh, and it was terrifying, too. Sira scrambled backward on her platform of ice until her back met a wall of water, soaking through her shirt. She didn't know what to do; if she simply fell through and ran, the Reaper might give chase, but if she stood her ground, she'd be disintegrated. Sira watched in horror as his hand began to reach through the now misty space towards her.

Olivia

"Spear him! I don't care how much you liked him!"

Therin blinked, but Olivia had asked so nicely, so surely that was what convinced her. The other girl turned upward and held up her telescopic spear, pointing it directly at the Reaper. It expanded, rocketing up to knock him squarely on the side of the head.

Olivia sent a semi-silent signal, *Now!*

As soon as she had seen Sira going in, she had known what was going to happen and had set up an attack plan. At her signal, Aly began gunning the Reaper from the other side, pelting him with shots all over in the opposite direction from which Therin's spear had come. Instead of knocking him into a spin like she'd hoped, he merely shook his head, like he'd gotten splashed with cold water. He raised his hand with his fingers gathered.

Olivia knew what he was going to do next; all overpowered characters did it when they were annoyed, *Sira, get out of there.*

In response, Olivia saw a wet lump of teenager push out of the water egg she'd formed. When the Reaper snapped, a swiftly expanding sphere of energy began at his fingertips. She raced against it, running in to catch Sira, whose fall seemed to slow as Olivia approached, then running back out, a heavy load of wet teenager on her back slowing her down considerably.

When she stopped, letting Sira's momentum carry her to the ground, Olivia saw that everything within a certain radius of the Reaper had been razed, even the demons that had been within the range of the snap. A few on the very border found half of their bodies singed to nothing before disappearing completely. Whoever the Reaper thought he was, he clearly had no regard for anything.

The monster brushed his hands as if they were dirty, "Whoops, clumsy me. I suppose I should be more careful with total annihilation, but at least I have a nice crater now."

"How are you going to fill it?!" A voice shouted from across the gray field. Olivia looked for its source and found Dom, hurling his jagged sword at the Reaper.

He caught it and the sword disintegrated, "Marshmallow cream. Though, I suppose if I can't," he thrust out his hand, shooting a burst of ethereal force at Dom, "I'll settle for your blood."

Olivia watched as Dom ran ahead of the continuous stream of Essence that churned the earth behind him. Wherever the attack landed, it left behind it a trail of glass, concocted by the ground and the demons unfortunate enough to be caught up in it.

The Reaper must have seen her, since he yelled a bit too cheerily to her, "Hey, don't feel left out! You can join in on the fun, too." His other hand pulsed on the far side of them, causing another spot of broiling land to form. Olivia took off, not having the time to grab Therin or Sira. She merely hoped they were ready to run.

They were being forced toward the other pulse, vice gripped between them. Dom signaled to his left, toward the Reaper. *All right,* Olivia replied, *might as well.* Moments before she and Dom reached the same point, she took off to her right at a square angle, taking a direct path towards their enemy.

She heard the churning behind her stop, so she gazed up to see the Reaper putting his hands down. "What, you didn't think I'd actually fall for that, did you?" Without waiting for a response, he divided evenly, splitting into two separate Reapers. He divided again and again until the sky was full of them, blocking their aerial escape from all directions. All of them sported a creepy smile. In unison, their voices resonated, sounding like thunder with so many, "Now this is more like it."

Olivia looked at how close together they were, even clustering in some places. She reached her hand into the pouch at her side, feeling the gritty powder. With a leap, she threw the powder into the air in an arc, directly hitting one of the Reapers. Instantly, he began to dissolve. The powder reached a couple of others and spread like a wildfire, ripping through the cloud of Reapers, liquefying them in moments.

All, of course, except for one. Even when the chain reaction reached him, he just floated there with an amused expression on his face. Olivia didn't care; at least they'd found the real one, even if he was a field away.

The Reaper waved his hand like he was saying hello, "You wanna know the best part about my clones?"

Olivia's heart skipped a beat, "What?"

"They can do anything I can."

As if on cue, the hordes of Reapers that had disappeared moments ago rematerialized, all laughing loudly, like they were just playing a game. It was terrifying.

All at once, the laughing stopped and Olivia sought their faces for a cause. They were all looking in on her and her friends with that creepy smile again. She looked around, seeing if the others were braced for the end. Dom was there, Sira was there. Ryan and Aly had caught up to them. They all looked like they were scared for their lives. But where was…?

Therin

As soon as the real Reaper had revealed himself, Therin disappeared, going under the visible radar. Invisible now, she ran as fast as she could, never taking her eyes off of him. Even when the clones revealed themselves again, she kept approaching. Therin reached a spot below him and jumped up to grab him.

The Reaper was hot to the touch, but Therin didn't care. Even as the other Reapers turned to her, aiming their unrelenting gaze at her, she didn't care. She could hear her friends yelling at her, demanding to know what she was doing. Even the Reaper, looking down at her clinging to his wrist, "What are you doing?"

Therin gritted her teeth, hating the sound of his voice with every ounce of her being, "Do you want the good line or the cliché one?"

"The cliché one, if you please."

A tear escaped Therin's eye as she leaped further up his body in order to embrace him completely, "Saving you."

She shut her eyes, but she could still feel the Reaper trembling. Perhaps it was his own shock, but they plummeted to the ground. When they hit the ground, Therin's head was jarred, but she didn't let go. She couldn't. Not if she could save Kyo. Watching the battle told Therin something; if the Reaper had the power to wipe everything out, the only reason he hadn't already was because Kyo was holding him back.

Suddenly, the Reaper started laughing beneath her, "It's amusing you think this will save you."

Therin sat up, putting as much pressure as she could on his stomach, trying to squeeze the air out of him, "If Kyo's still in there, I can bring him out."

The Reaper laughed harder, apparently unfazed by Therin's pressure, "Kyo's my body. If you bring him out like this, that proves he's a pervert."

"I don't care if he's a pervert!"

The Reaper blinked, his eyes now wide, fearful, "Now, now, there's no need to--"

"Do you know why?!" Therin screamed, "It's because I... because I..."

"What, because you love him? You're a little young to know about love, aren't you?" He sat up, pushing Therin aside onto the ground. Now he stood over her, "Just because you pretend to love him doesn't mean you can save him. In case you forget, I'm his mind, and I don't love you."

In response, Therin leapt up and kissed him on the lips. She had to stand on her toes, but she could kiss him. That was all she needed.

The Reaper pulled away. Therin was glad to see she wasn't the only one blushing, "Why...? What was--"

"I didn't kiss you, you jerk."

His eyes bulged, full of terror. His mouth twitched, then his hand. Then he collapsed on the ground and began to writhe. All of the clones that were still lingering in the air faded away, as if they had never existed. Therin knelt down next to him, watching him twist and contort into unnatural positions. She was scared, worried that she'd made things worse. Would the conflict kill him? If it did, would she be okay with that, knowing that it would have set him free?

Therin kept watching him, tears falling steadily now, as the others trotted up. Dom knelt and touched the Reaper's forehead, whether to check for a fever or as comfort, Therin had no idea. He was still having a seizure, fighting himself inside and out. She could only think of one thing to do. She hugged him again.

This time, he froze, his arms and legs stayed in a frightening pose. Then she could feel him relax. Therin didn't let him go, even as he lay completely still. He didn't move.

Therin couldn't believe it. After all that hard work, the Reaper took him from her. That wasn't right. Kyo was hers. He belonged to her. And she belonged to him. All the times that she had talked to him, looked up to him, laughed with him. Every time, she could see someone powerful, someone she could trust. And now he was… He was…

She felt an arm around her back. Then another, tightening now. Therin pulled out of her hug and looked at Kyo's face. It was still different than before, but he was there, in control. The way he looked at her, gazed into her eyes. It made no difference that his eyes were no longer black, that his hair was no longer a raven's nest, he was still the same.

Therin reinforced her hug, holding his neck tight, never wanting to let go. Her tears weren't for grief anymore. Now they fell onto the ground because she was happy. She was beyond happy, she was euphoric. Therin listened to the laughter of her companions as she sat back from Kyo and let him have a turn speaking to everyone. Their happiness could not compare.

Kyo

Waking up in a strange body was nothing new, but waking up with Therin hugging him, the scent of her furry wolf ears like a stuffed animal, that was new. When Kyo hugged her back, she could feel her stiffen. When she pulled away to look at him, she could see her closer than ever. She'd brought him back, even as his mind kept pulling him away.

His mind was a lot stronger now. Kyo could think about so many things in an instant. And his heartbeat felt so real. Was that really a crystal merely pretending to be a heart? Or, since it was combined with Anima and Animus, was it complete? And he could talk now. His voice was strange to him, but he gladly used it to greet his friends.

But even with everything new to distract him, he couldn't shake his nagging headache. It had started as soon as he had woken up. Even as Kyo was talking to everyone, he looked inside himself, searching for what he knew was still there.

Miss me, did you?
How are you still alive?

I'm your mind, of course. Even though you have some control over me right now, you still can't seem to grasp that.

Get out of here.

If only I could. Unfortunately for you, the only way I can't be here is if I'm in control.

So that means I'm safe. Good.

Hardly. Even now, I'm working my way back out. Your tie to this little girl is weak. It's weird that both of you think that romance is possible, anyway.

So the only way to get rid of you is to--

Kill us both, yes. But since I know you don't have the strength, you couldn't possibly do that. Besides, what would Therin think?

Kyo didn't reply. He'd already made his decision. Best to carry it out without anyone knowing. He stopped talking and put his hand on his chest, channeling all his power into it.

Therin's hands snatched his. He looked up into her eyes, "Whatever you're doing, stop."

Kyo couldn't bear it. He let all of his tears go, felt them flow down his cheeks. When he spoke, it was flawed and halting, "If I don't, the Reaper can come back."

"He-he can't. He's gone." Her eyes started leaking, too.

Kyo shook his head. She got the message and she started crying forcefully again. Watching her like this was unbearable, so he embraced her, pulling her into his shoulder. She kept on crying, soaking his shoulder. He didn't care. He just felt a little guilty for soaking hers.

Pulling away was impossible, but Kyo managed to do it. He wanted the moment to last forever, but he knew that he obeyed the laws of time and that the Reaper would undoubtedly break free if he let it. He felt his piercing headache spike and knew he had mere moments.

Kyo glance at everyone else one last time, silently saying his goodbyes. Dom, Ryan, Olivia, Sira, and even Aly had left quite an impression on him. And especially Therin. He just hoped that they would remember him when they woke up. He knew they would now, since the only thing tying them to Dream was him, the Reaper. It was a cruel joke of Anima's to tie their life forces to it so that they couldn't leave until it was destroyed.

And now it would be. Kyo didn't hesitate this time, even when Therin desperately tugged at his arm, trying to pull his glowing hand away from his chest. He felt the Essence leave his fingers and weave its way into the fabric of his being. His Essence would try to heal him, but he would overload it.

Kyo began to tear himself apart. Bit by bit, he could feel it working, the farthest part of him fading first. As his Essence faded, he threw every last bit of it at himself, so that he couldn't regenerate. He felt water fall into his eyes while he stared up at Therin, her head directly over his. Soon that image faded away, leaving only blackness. That was how he started. He might as well end that way.

Epilogue

Aly watched as Kyo faded away, Therin's arms phasing through his body as if it wasn't even there. As he faded, she could feel her senses slipping. The gray grass around them, the fallen bodies of the demons, the rubble, all of it started to be consumed by some kind of black rush. But Aly didn't mind. All she wanted to do was sleep. So she did, closed her eyes just before the darkness reached her.

Finally, Aly was calm, floating in the darkness. She wondered if this was what Kyo was talking about in his memories. Perhaps, but she had no way of knowing. At the very least, it meant that she was... what? Aly didn't know. For all she knew, Dream had destroyed itself and now she was stuck in limbo. But no, that couldn't be it. This felt too much like a lucid dream. But hadn't the whole thing felt like a lucid dream? So if it was now, all she had to do was...

Aly sat upright in her hospital bed, awake. She was dizzy, but quickly got over it. Looking around, she saw that the equipment that surrounded her bed was new, beeping at different rhythms and showing numbers that meant nothing to her. But none of that was as important as Zach and Ave standing there in her room.

"What are you guys doing here?" She asked, curious.

Zach blinked, apparently surprised, "U-um, visiting?"

Aly raised an eyebrow. Something was up, "Well, are you?" She looked at Ave behind him. They were both dressed weird, wearing black cloaks or something like that. She could see Zach wearing that kind of thing; he was emo enough. But Ave?

The taller girl just shrugged. Aly looked at the clock, "It's two in the morning!"

"I'm not stalking you if that's what you're implying," Zach replied.

Aly didn't even know what she was implying, "Then what are you doing?"

"It'd take a while to explain."

She looked at her hospital bracelet, "I've got time."

I hung up the phone. Sira had really gone into detail. Which was good, considering her side of the story had a longer and more complete timeline than Aly's did. Of course, I had recorded the whole thing, not knowing whether or not it would come in handy later on. The whole thing was really interesting. To think that I was having similar dreams the whole time.

Some things in her account of it conflicted with Aly, but that was to be expected, since they were two different people. I didn't care. All that mattered was that I got the whole story. Of course, since Sira was so behind on her creative writing homework, I suggested that she use it as her assignment material. Granted, I'd never be able to use it without her direct permission, but that was the price to pay for being a nice guy.

One thing didn't make any sense whatsoever. It had been only two days since she and everyone had woken up, but one of the players was standing right next to me and had been for the past week. In fact, Dom had never been in a coma the entire time I'd known him.

"What is it, Zach?" He asked.

"Oh, nothing really."

"Upset you had to leave Aly back at the hospital?"

"No, that's not it. I'm just trying to figure something out," I explained, deliberately keeping it vague in hope that he'd leave me alone.

"All right, then."

Good. Masterful conversation skills are useful, after all.

But if Dom was right here, does that mean that Anima just picked up another random Dom from somewhere in the world? No, that was unlikely; I'd asked Sira to describe him as he appeared to her and the description was spot on. So, unless he had a doppelgänger that had the same name… Ugh, it was all so complicated. The only other explanation was… no, but I'd know if something like that happened. It wasn't that, trust me. Whatever you might think, reader, it certainly wasn't that.

Except for the fact that *they* were here. *They* might give me just the evidence I needed for such a hypothesis. Of course, if *they* wanted to introduce themselves, I wouldn't be using the pronoun game. But it was interesting how their weapons showed up in Sira's story about Dream. I'd have to think about it some more.

Therin sighed. This was her third day out of the hospital, a week and a half since she'd woken up. Since she was "feeling better", she might as well go with Ryan and Erin to musical theater. Since she hadn't had a dream of Kyo since, she was giving up on ever seeing him again. Guess he really was a dream after all.

Hopping out of the car, Therin realized just how normal everything felt. She'd never be the same way again. She could see it in Ryan, too. Sure, he was happy, but he got bored a lot more easily now. Of course, she'd always had issues paying attention, but now she found herself drifting off into a daydream every now and then, thinking about…

No, if he didn't exist, Therin shouldn't think about him. Not at all. Whether it was with his calm black eyes and wild black hair or the blue eyes and equally wild brown hair. She hit her head with the heel of her hand, "Stop it!" She whispered out loud.

"Stop what?" asked Ryan.

"Not you."

Therin walked inside without another thought, not even waving goodbye to mom. The older class was just getting out, chatting and singing based on whatever the song they'd worked on today. It gave no clues to Therin; they were all doing completely different songs for the showcase, anyway. For the most part, she kept her eyes down, not really in the mood to make eye contact.

She saw an oddly shaped pair of bare feet, poised on the toes, like a cat. Therin recognized them, but kept walking. She felt a hand grab her shoulder and she stopped, looking at her brother with contempt. Ryan didn't say anything, he just pointed at the table.

At it was sitting Zach, his feet pointing inward on the high stool. She caught his eyes for a brief moment, but he looked away, the blank look on his face unchanged. A crazy hat covered his brown hair, as usual, but something was different about him. It wasn't the hair, the bare feet, his blue eyes, all of that was normal. No, what was different was… he didn't look… tired.

It clicked. Therin almost started crying again, but it was time for class.

Warning

The following story may be disturbing to some readers

Reader discretion is advised

Sentaku

Jamie hopped out of the van with all the energy that had been stored during the short car ride to the park. The only other car in the lot was a black car, so it looked like he might have the whole playground to himself. He pushed the button to close the automatic door and jumped up and down in impatient excitement as his mother climbed out of the driver's seat. "C'mon, I wanna go play on the slides!"

"Believe me, Jamie, I can tell." Mom replied as she walked around him to grab stuff from the trunk.

His fifteen-year-old sister, Margie, came around from the front seat, "Do you want me to take care of Paul, then?" She asked it rather huffily, like she was in a poor mood.

Mom didn't notice, "If you would, that would be great. Just make sure to keep him out of the snacks until we all have some."

With that, Mom gently grabbed Jamie's hand and started towards the pavilion in the park. Jamie desperately pulled to make Mom go faster so they could set up base and he could get to playing at once, but besides a few quick stumbles, he was unable to get her to go any faster. At long last, he stepped off of the neatly trimmed grass and onto the smooth concrete that was cool to the touch, due to the shady roof above it. It was the perfect place to see the whole playground of the park below and the track around for bikers and walkers.

Mom rolled out some soft blankets on the metal picnic tables to mark their places and to make the seats more comfortable. Just as she was finished spreading out,

Jamie heard a scream that was undoubtedly Paul's. He turned to see that the three-year-old was thrashing in Margie's arms. She had wisely placed the picnic basket in the hand restraining his arms, so his pumping legs were unable to harm their food.

As soon as Mar had put Paul down and safely stowed the basket on top of the table, Mom turned Jamie loose to play. He bolted from the cover of the pavilion as fast as his seven-year-old legs could take him. He leapt over the short black divider between the grass and the mulch of the playground. Skirting the jungle gym, he ran straight for the large playhouse. Wanting to challenge himself, he started to climb up the pole that had layered steps all the way up. When he reached the top, Jamie gazed around the playground from his vantage point. Not a lot of kids were here today, but maybe that was because they were homeschooled and it was cloudy anyways.

Jamie looked at the pavilion. Paul was apparently pouting. Very loudly. Jamie could hear him from where he was. Mar looked bored, thumbing through her phone with her headphones in while Mom desperately tried to quiet down Paul. Jamie shrugged it off. That just meant no one was watching him and he could do whatever he wanted. Without another thought, he launched himself down the tunneled slide.

After the curving, dark ride, the thrilling bumps and turns throughout the whole thing bringing laughs to his mouth, he came out into the gentle, cloudy light. He sat up on the end of the slide and nearly jumped when he saw the man standing next to it. The man was big and dressed like he was going somewhere nice for dinner. Jamie hated wearing those kinds of shirts. Especially when Mom made him wear a tie for Church.

He was leaning against the slide when he asked Jamie, "Hey, kid, how's it going?"

Not wanting to be rude, Jamie replied, "Fine."

He got up and latched onto the climbing wall in the middle of the park. He couldn't see Mom anymore, but he was pretty good at getting to the top. Jamie heard the man's footsteps behind him. He was wary of the man, though he didn't know why, so he started climbing to the top fast as he could.

The man stopped under him and spoke again, "Where's your family?"

Jamie straddled the top of the wall and pointed to the pavilion, "My mom is over there."

The man peeked through one of the holes for stepping in the wall, "What about your dad?"

"At work," Jamie shrugged, "He never really comes to play with us."

"Do you want me to play with you?" The man asked nicely. Perhaps he wasn't so scary after all.

Jamie thought about it briefly before nodding.

"All right, then how about you come down and we can go do the swings?"

Jamie nodded again, "Sure!"

He started to climb down again, carefully stepping from foothold to foothold. As soon as his feet touched the ground, he felt a cloth press against his nose and mouth. It smelled sharp, but sweet. After just a sniff, Jamie's eyes felt heavy. Just before he fell asleep, he could see the man smiling as the little boy fell on the ground.

Jamie didn't know how long it had been. He knew that this third house he was in, a man's, had paid even more money than the last. It had been like this for a while since the man in the playground had kidnapped and sold him. Since then, people had done. . . horrible things to him. He was pretty sure they were evil, because he hurt everywhere, but mostly in his pants. Some things just throbbed, but outside of his clothing, there were bruises that hurt constantly. This new man really liked to hurt him. He was much worse than the last lady, who forgot to feed him sometimes.

Jamie lived in an upstairs room with another slave. She was quiet and had never said her name. She looked a bit older than him, but not as old as Mar. Jamie tried not to think of Mar too often, since he cried then. Sometimes, when the man was done with her, he just chained her up without any clothes, so she was all red and covered in bruises. Jamie always tried to look away when that happened. The worst times were when the man didn't do the bad things to either of them, but made them do it to each other. Jamie shook his head, trying to erase it from his thoughts.

He heard heavy footsteps coming up the stairs. Jamie shifted uncomfortably in his chains, wondering what was going to happen. The man reached the top of the stairs and immediately went over to the girl, pulling out the key to her cuffs. Jamie watched as the girl began to cry silently as the metal rings fell to the ground and were replaced by a firm grip that wouldn't allow her to escape.

The man's phone rang and with his free hand, he put away his key and answered his cell phone. As he began talking, Jamie looked down; he probably had another torturous hour in which he would pretend not to hear what was going on downstairs, but he really could hear, as the man's bedroom was directly under this room. He closed his eyes and, despite his discomfort, tried to fall asleep, shutting out the man talking.

He heard a dull thud on the carpet in front of him and he opened his eyes to see what it was. Jamie tried not to gasp when he saw that it was a key. He looked up to see the girl looking back at him, tears in her eyes as the man was still talking on his phone while leading her down the stairs. She didn't want to be freed, she just wanted Jamie to get out.

With his limited reach, Jamie grabbed the key and waited until he heard the bedroom door close downstairs. It was awkward, trying to unlock his own handcuffs, but after a bit of fumbling, he heard the satisfying click of freedom. The rings dropped away from his wrists and dully thudded on the carpeted floor. He winced at each sound, as he was afraid the man might hear him. So far, no angry footsteps were racing upstairs.

Jamie crept down the hallway to the stairs on all fours, crawling silently. When he reached the stairwell, he stood up, more than a little shakily. He latched onto the handrail and took the first step. It creaked a little, but it wasn't a loud sound. Jamie kept walking down the stairs.

Near the bottom, he was overwhelmed by a wave of vertigo and he collapsed. He could feel himself roll down the remaining stairs and he knew, when he was he was back to his senses on the bottom, that he had been loud. The man's footsteps could be heard in the bedroom, coming towards his door. Jamie looked around for the front door, but he couldn't find it. With no other choice, he started back up the stairs again, this time pushed by a rush of adrenaline.

When the bedroom door slammed open, the man yelled a word Jamie had heard several times since his kidnapping. It made him want to run faster. When he got to the top of the stairs, he could hear the man behind him, so he bolted down the hallway, hoping to find someplace to hide. No doubt he'd be killed or sold for this. Jamie wasn't sure what'd be worse.

On his left, just before the hallway ended, there was another stairwell, this one ending at a door. Jamie leapt up the stairs and tried the door. It was unlocked. He was met with something he hadn't seen in a very long time, sunlight. He was on the roof of the building. Perhaps, if he could get to the edge before the man got to him, he could climb down and escape.

Jamie ran for the wall at the border of the rooftop and looked down. The building was much higher than he expected, but he couldn't let fear stop him from escaping. He found where a drainpipe was and straddled the wall, grabbing onto the pipe for support. He heard a yell from the direction of the door and he turned to see the man, angrily panting in the doorway. Jamie seized up in fear, his hands reflexively pulling up to protect his chest.

He lost his balance.

Jamie fell from the building, wind rushing past his ears. He looked up. Or rather, down. The pavement on the street was fast approaching. Perhaps Jamie did know what was better, after all. He closed his eyes just as he was swallowed in light.

When he opened them, he was on the pavilion. Paul was pouting, Mar was getting out her headphones, and Mom was trying different things to cheer up Paul.

Out loud, Jamie asked, "What?"

Mom responded, "I said you can go and play if you want."

Jamie blinked. After all he had been through, had it all been a dream? But it couldn't be. He'd never even heard of the things that had happened to him. But he still remembered it all. Could it be that he had a second chance? He looked at the parking lot, and saw the black car. He shivered with aversion.

"Actually, Mom, I think I'll stay here for a little while to help out."

Mom raised an eyebrow, but immediately set him to work getting Paul out of his fit. Jamie genuinely smiled as Mar ignored everything, as Paul eventually started laughing at Jamie's tickles, and as Mom had some time to breathe. Most of all, Jamie watched with pleasure as this time, the first man, the one who had kidnapped him, walked to his black car with a frustrated look and drove away.

Made in the USA
Lexington, KY
22 September 2019